3 MARBLES

A Novel by
JAN R. MCDONALD

• Chicago •

3 Marbles
A Novel by
Jan R. McDonald

Published by
Joshua Tree Publishing
• Chicago •
JoshuaTreePublishing.com

All rights reserved. No part of this book may be reproduced or transmitted in any form or by any means, electronic or mechanical, including information storage and retrieval system without written permission from the publisher, except by a reviewer who may quote brief passages in a review.

13-Digit ISBN Print: 978-1-956823-17-2
13-Digit ISBN eBook: 978-1-956823-98-1
Copyright © 2022. Jan R. McDonald All Rights Reserved.

Front Cover Image Credit: Couple: keleny - stock.adobe.com
Background Cover Credit: Photo by illu - depositphotos.com

Disclaimer:
This is a work of fiction. Names, characters, places, and incidents are the product of the author's imagination or have been used fictitiously. Any resemblance to actual persons, living or dead, events, locales or organizations is entirely coincidental.

Printed in the United States of America

Dedication
To

COURTNEY, PARKER AND TAYLOR MCDONALD WHO ALLOWED ME TO BE A STORYTELLER

Chapter 1

Three-year-old Alex lay motionless under the metal bedframe. A thin blanket hung over the side of the bed, hiding him from sight. The single bedroom was usually a busy place but not today. It was hot, damp, and dusty, and he tried not to breathe in too much of the dust and dirt from the wooden floor. He listened carefully for changes to the sounds from outside, waiting to see if they would get quiet or louder. Above him, a spider busily spun new webs in hopes of catching the dusty insects dislodged by the boy.

He heard a door bang outside. Men were yelling, and he recognized Philippe's voice but not the others. He heard the sound of a shot, then two more. Silence followed, then low voices talking. Silence again. Seconds later, a car motor started up loudly, then grew quieter as it got farther away. The boy knew what would come next; soon, the screaming and crying would begin. He had heard these sounds before.

Alex heard his mother call his name quietly. She said he could come out from under the bed. He crawled out and went down the stairs to where his mother was waiting in the living room. His father was by the window, making sure none of Beltrán's men were still there.

"Ve con Ava, asegúrate de que ella esté bien, amore," Alex's father said over his shoulder. ("Make sure Ava is OK.") His mother quickly went to the back of the house, closing the noisy screen door behind her as she walked across the yard to check on their neighbor's wife Ava.

Chilapa was a beautiful place. Surrounded by lush green mountains and bright golden flowers, the beauty hid its terrible past and present. Long established as the gateway to the poppy production zone, the area was controlled by a branch of the Sinaloa Cartel run by the Beltrán brothers.

The town existed only to work the fields for the cartel that ran it with an iron fist. There were no choices; you did as you were told, or you disappeared. Even young children were forced to work in the fields. Lately, because of President Zedillo's military crackdown on drug trafficking, tensions were higher than normal, and death was becoming a too-familiar part of life.

That night, Alex listened from his bed as his parents talked quietly in theirs. The single bedroom left little space for privacy, and Alex had learned to ignore things that didn't concern him. Tonight, however, he could sense the seriousness of their talk, and he felt something he had not felt before—their fear.

Morning came quickly. Normally, the labor bus was in town just as the sun broke through the mountains, but this morning, a delay had made the bus late. The villagers were lined up to board it as usual—all of the men, women, and children of the village. Only the sick or infirm were allowed to stay in their houses, and the drug growers searched each one to make sure there were no slackers. The guards from the bus had a tally sheet, but it wasn't accurate since they never bothered to update it after the killings. The town had several families with young sons like Alex, and that included his neighbor who had been killed the night before.

Alex was dressed and standing by the door, ready to go outside, but his father grabbed his arm.

"Rápidamente, ven conmigo pero sé muy callado." ("Come with me quickly, but be very quiet.") He pulled Alex into the kitchen, where his mother was climbing outside through the window. He motioned for Alex to follow her, and he did as he was told, going out through the window behind her. He half-climbed and half-fell out of the kitchen, but his mother caught him, and then his father came out behind them, still not saying why they were doing this.

Señor Della was outside waiting for them behind the house, and he motioned for them to follow him. Although he was curious, Alex sensed that now was not the time to question his parents.

Ernesto Della was a delivery driver for the drug traffickers and, as such, had more freedom to travel than most. What his employers didn't realize was that for the right price, Ernesto would smuggle people out of Chilapa in the false bottom of his old truck. With the increase in killings, his business was booming.

It was a tight fit for the three of them under the false truck bottom, and the hot exhaust fumes were overpowering until the truck started moving. For a time, they traveled down the two-lane highway that connects Chilapa de Alvarez and Chilpancingo, the capital of Guerrero, Mexico. Finally reaching the city center, Ernesto took them to the Zócalo, where the artists and craftsmen plied their trades during the day and went home to hide at night. The old truck stopped in an alley, partially blocked by wooden fruit crates stacked against the brick walls on either side. The old engine died, and Ernesto quietly told them to stay still while he made their connections for the rest of the trip.

While they waited, Alex finally had to ask, "¿Que hacemos, mammá?" ("What are we doing, Mama?") Alex turned his head to face his mother.

"Nos vamos de, mi hijo. Nos vamos a vivir a los Estados Unidos donde sea seguro." ("We are leaving, my son. We are going to the United States to live where it will be safe.")

What they didn't know then was that in a matter of days, Alex would be without a home or a father.

Chapter 2

Three stories up on the roof of the old gray building, the hot El Paso wind whistled through wooden pallets and shipping crates. They were stacked haphazardly on the softening tar and gravel roof as if a giant had gotten tired of playing with them and dropped them in a pile. The hot summer air was filled with dust and industrial smells. Inside the pile of rotting wood, a small space housed a seven-year-old boy scrunched back into the shadows as far as he could go. The boy felt sharp stabs from the splintered wood and rusty nails against his arms and back, but he ignored it. The air was thick with the smell of creosote from the pallets and the stink of some rotting animal close to his hiding place. The boy's skin was the same weathered brown color as the decaying pallets and crates, and unless he moved, he was just another piece of weathered wood in the pile. The boy figured that as long as he was quiet inside the pile, he'd be OK.

Alex listened to the kids yelling taunts and threats outside the stack and tried not to choke on the thick, dirty air. He pulled his Power Ranger T-shirt up over his nose and took shallow breaths. He hated being under the rotting wood, but it was safe here. None of the kids outside would try to crawl underneath the pile to get him out.

The boys hunting Alex were from one of the groups of street children living on the El Paso streets near a bridge crossing to Juarez, Mexico. The old slum area had become a home for immigrant children and a few adults living off the grid. Even El Paso's homeless community shunned this part of town and its lack of opportunity. The old, abandoned buildings had become makeshift camps, some housing up to a dozen boys and girls, mostly ranging from three to fifteen years old. All were survivors of some illegal border crossing or escape from society. Many had lost their parents to ICE (International Customs Enforcement) agents and some to the violence of the border crossings. Most hoped they were there only for a short time, hiding in the buildings, waiting for their parents to come get them. Others knew that would never happen and tried to make a life there on the streets. All wanted to stay out of sight of the authorities in this ignored section of town.

To survive, the orphaned kids had formed groups in order to help each other stay alive. Most of the groups had at least one adult who tried to manage their welfare as best they could. The kids were constantly watched by the drug runners doing business several blocks away. The children too weak or too young to contribute or survive on their own were taken by the gangs who controlled the lower slum areas. They were offered for sale or were disposed of. When the kids reached fifteen or looked close to it, they were taken into the gangs to become runners and mules for their drug businesses. The girls were used as prostitutes or kept by the gangs for their members. The young children they didn't want just disappeared.

Alex was luckier than most; he still had his mother. The kids disliked him because he was a loner, living in an old, abandoned apartment with his mother instead of the groups like them. Somehow, he had found a way to survive without their help, which made them suspicious. He always seemed to have food, which they envied because there was never enough food for the groups, even though the drug gangs dropped off care packages every week.

The kids older than Alex were the meanest because they had the most to prove. They had to show their worth to the drug traffickers who were always watching them. The boys wanted to become gang members when they were old enough because the gangs always had food, good clothes, and even a little money. Alex listened as the group boys left the roof. He listened to them shuffle through the gravel and debris. They got bored quickly if they didn't find him right away, and they would go off to find easier prey.

He could hear them laughing and stomping on his toys as they left, leaving signs of their superiority. Alex sat and waited in the hot dark for another ten minutes. Sometimes group boys stayed behind, hoping he'd crawl out from under one of the debris piles so they could grab him. They had caught him twice this way last year, and he had the scars from those mistakes.

The kids didn't really hate him for any particular reason. Alex was a loner, so he was distrusted, and distrust meant frequent beatings. He was just something for them to do. Alex listened but only heard the sheet metal scraping on the old downspouts and the singing of the hot wind in the rusted pipes. He didn't expect anyone to still be there; he wasn't worth more than a few minutes of their time.

He rolled from his rear end to his knees, but his T-shirt caught on a nail sticking out of a pallet, and he was snagged. He reached back and unhooked it, scraping his arm on the rough wood. The debris he was under gave him just enough room to sit. If they ever shifted while he was under here, the pile would crush him instantly, but he still felt safer here in the dark hole than on the open roof. The group kids were too big or too scared of the spiders and rats or the collapse to come in after him. Alex preferred the dark, rodents, and insects to the boys. In another year or two, he'd be too big to fit in here, and he'd have to find another place to hide—or stand and fight them. He had tried to fight them twice last year when they caught him, but he was too little and too weak. They beat him badly both times, but the beatings didn't bother him too much. After the first few punches and kicks, he didn't really feel them until afterward, but his mom couldn't handle it. The boys had hurt her more than him.

The wind was still blowing hot and dirty when Alex crawled out and stood up, looking around the sunbaked roof. No one was in sight on the flat roof, just trash and broken pieces of his two action figures thrown down near the old air handlers. The toys didn't matter to Alex; he could use sticks or rocks to play with. He felt in his right pants pocket for the three marbles. The boys would take them if they caught him, even though he'd fight to keep them, but today it looked like he wouldn't have to.

Alex quietly slipped off the roof, the softened tar and rocks sticking to his old worn sneakers. He went down the steps through the old factory to the side door and headed back to the abandoned tenant building where he lived with his mom. A neighbor had told his mom that Alex was like a little rat, sneaking around the deserted buildings looking for food. But the rats lived pretty well in his building, thought Alex, so he didn't mind.

They lived in the old part of El Paso, close to the US-Mexican border crossing. It was a regular stopping place for illegal immigrants sneaking into the States because there wasn't much border security here. A few blocks away, the border gangs held shop for city residents who came down looking to score drugs or girls. The cops and ICE rarely came down to this part of town because there was nothing of interest for them in the crumbling warehouses and apartment buildings. More than one rotting corpse could be found in the old buildings, but no one paid much attention. Several times, Alex had almost tripped over a body decomposing and covered with maggots in some deserted hallway. He was used to the death that lived in this part of town, and he would just step over the body and move on.

A few families lived in the dilapidated buildings, and the ones that did squatted in abandoned apartments, some with wires strung out through second-story windows to old power poles. The squatters were homeless immigrants like him and his mother, and they lived on what they could find or steal. Small groups of feral children also roamed the old buildings, looking for anything that could be sold or traded. The younger group kids were picked on by both the older kids and the traffickers who took anything of value that the younger kids found or stole. Most of the children joined a group for protection and food, but Alex was an exception. The children attended the school of life here; there was no formal education because that would mean being on the grid.

A few of the kids had a parent or two and just hung around the groups during the day, but the majority were orphans. To avoid the system, they stayed in the old buildings and lived on the streets, which was preferable to being picked up by the police, child protective services, or ICE agents. They all knew the stories of children who were picked up and processed. They ended up in detention, sometimes hidden from their real parents to force them to cooperate. Most of the street kids would rather take their chances with each other than trust the authorities with their lives. Again, Alex felt for the three marbles his father had given him. They were always in his pocket for reassurance. He didn't remember why they were so important, but he knew that they were, and he hung on to the marbles like a safety net.

Chapter 3

The three older boys had cornered nine-year-old Alex in the basement of a deserted apartment building. They positioned themselves so he couldn't run past them through the only door to the room. Alex stared at them silently as they taunted him with insults about his father and mother. The smallest of them outweighed him by at least twenty pounds, and the other two were even bigger. Alex guessed that they were eleven or twelve, old enough to want to look good for the ever-watchful gangs. They figured Alex would be an easy beating, one they could brag about to the older boys.

He had grown a lot in the last year, although he was still small compared to them. He didn't have an ounce of fat on him, a product of a limited diet and a lot of exercise. What he did have was a strength much greater than most children his age and a complete lack of fear. He knew this day would come, and he had spent the last year getting ready for it.

Brian, the oldest and, by default, the leader of their little group, squared his shoulders. He didn't like the fact that the kid wasn't moved to run or fight by their taunts, but he'd just take it out on him with his feet and fists. The kid was weird anyway, never talking to the group kids and running around the old buildings like a dog. It was time to teach him who ruled the streets down here. Brian heard a noise and saw his friends move back to stand by the doorway to watch. *Good*, he thought, *I'll give them a real show.*

Brian fainted with a left jab to Alex's face, which usually made a kid cover up. Then he would then use his feet to bring the kid down, but this kid didn't move his hands up—he just moved out of range of the fist.

"Screw it," Brian thought and waded in with both fists flying. But he never touched the little kid and somehow ended up on the ground, bleeding from his lips.

Randy and Eric jumped in to help their friend, and within seconds, both were on the ground with Brian. Then the little kid did the unthinkable—he began beating them with his fists and feet as they lay on the ground. There was an audible crack as Eric's arm bone snapped from a kick, and he cried out in agony. Other kids in the street, drawn by the screams, ran up to watch the carnage. They were shocked to see the bigger kids on the ground crying and the vicious little kid attacking them. The girl with the group screamed at Alex to stop, placing herself between the hurt boys and Alex. She didn't like the three boys on the ground, but the little kid looked like he wasn't going to stop hurting them.

Alex stopped and stared at her, breathing hard. She noticed his T-shirt and faded jeans, conscious of the fact that they looked cleaner than her own. He was a few inches shorter than her, and his eyes looked wild and his hair sticking up in all directions. Julia had just seen how dangerous he was and didn't know what he might do next. His fists were still clenched, and she was afraid he would hit her. Instead, he abruptly turned away and calmly walked past the other kids, not saying a word.

Chapter 4

After Alex beat Brian and his friends, the group kids stayed away from him. The drug gangs were curious about him, but he wasn't old enough to be of any use to them. They ignored him for the time being, but he was on their radar. Julia, the girl who had seen Alex in action, kept her distance also, although she was interested in him. From time to time, they would pass each other from the opposite sides of the street. They always stared at each other for a few seconds but never spoke. Still, both were aware of some sort of interest, but neither could define what that meant.

Julia was twelve and a half now, and her body had matured enough to draw interest from the older boys. She always wore clothes that were too large and a black beanie pulled down low to hide her long hair and attractive features. She was careful to stay in the background so as not to draw attention to herself. So far, it had worked, but she was watchful because two of the older boys seemed a little too interested in her movements.

Julia had also become a good fighter in her own right and had proven it several times with an older girl and two boys who had confronted her. The group boys knew about her toughness and preferred just to wait for the right time. Nobody was going anywhere.

Chapter 5

Near sundown, Alex walked ten dangerous blocks to where a local eatery served cheap Mexican food. He snuck back behind the restaurant and watched from a corner of the building as one of the workers smoked in the alley.

"Eduardo, venga aqui!" someone shouted through the screen door. Eduardo ground out the cigarette and went back inside, muttering. Alex took the opportunity to run to the dumpster. The lid was up, and he rummaged through the spoiled food and garbage and grabbed what he thought they could eat. He left quickly, flitting from shadow to shadow as the sun slowly made its way down from the sky. It was full dark by the time he got home.

Back at their apartment building, Alex quietly went in through the old lobby to the back stairs. There hadn't been electricity to the apartments for years, so the elevator was just another house for rats. Multiple families inhabited the apartments, so Alex was careful as he went down the hallway to their bottom-floor rooms. He tried the door, but it was locked. He had a key for the door, and he took it out and unlocked it. Their apartment had two electric lights because an old neighbor had illegally run wires out to the power pole where the old electric meter used to be. He was surprised that a light wasn't on to dispel the gloom.

"Madre, porque no luces?" he called out, entering the dark kitchen. He saw her silhouette on the floor and rushed over to her prone figure, reaching down to touch her face. Her skin was cold, and dull eyes stared up at him. Alex sat back on his haunches, looking at her. He reached into his pocket, feeling the three marbles, hoping for some comfort from them, but they didn't help. He had to think about what to do. He sat there for a long time in the dark. He didn't want to turn on the light because he didn't want to look at her. Finally, he made a decision. He stood up slowly, his legs numb from sitting in one position for so long. As feeling returned, he moved into the living room to where a threadbare rug covered the floor. He dragged it into the kitchen and unfolded it. Getting his hands under her armpits, he raised her up, dragged her onto the rug, and rolled her up in it. Not sure what to do next, he stood there trying to figure it out. He couldn't leave her here, and he had no way to bury her. If he just put her in the basement, the rats would get at her, and he didn't want that. He finally decided to put her in the old gas burner in the basement. It was steel and had doors he could close to keep the rats out. That was the best he could come up with.

After two hours of straining effort, Alex came back into the apartment. He wasn't concerned with taking care of himself, and for the past year, he had mostly taken care of her. Up to now, he hadn't had time to mourn or be sad, but with his immediate tasks done, he reverted to an eleven-year-old boy who had just lost his mother. It only lasted for a few minutes.

Chapter 6

Julia decided to go to the free market on a Saturday. This was a place where all the group kids could go without fear of attack because the gangs managed the gathering and violence wasn't allowed—except by them, of course. Street kids from all over old El Paso came with whatever they had to trade. Julia had some soap bars and an old basket she hoped to trade for vegetables or some not-too-rotten fruit. She entered the old warehouse and waited by the door until her eyes adjusted to the dim light. There was gambling and trading going on, and the sounds of laughter and cries of failure were loud. She had no interest in the games and walked straight over to the vegetable and fruit stands. Sharon had some tomatoes that weren't too overripe, and Don had a couple of apples. She haggled with them over the soap bars, and Don agreed to trade one apple for two bars of soap. Sharon wasn't interested. Julia took the deal and put the apple in her basket.

Not finding a trade for the basket, Julia decided to leave, preferring the outdoors to the stuffy warehouse. As she turned to leave, she noticed the boy Alex standing in the shadows near the door and, on a sudden impulse, walked directly toward him. He never took his eyes off her. Group kids had learned to talk in short sentences, almost a language of their own, and Julia realized she'd have to initiate the conversation. She turned and leaned against the metal wall, looking out at the busy room.

"Crowded," she said, not turning to look at him. She waited to see if he would respond. Then, after a few seconds, he did.

"Smells," he said, looking straight ahead. The protocol had been served.

"Julia," she said.

"Alex," he said.

They already knew each other's names, but this was a formal introduction. Again, protocol. Julia took the apple out of her basket and wiped it on her jacket. She took a bite, and this time, Alex turned to watch her. She kept looking straight ahead. One thing he remembered about her was how white and straight her teeth were. He was pleased to see they were still nice. She took another bite and chewed slowly. Then she turned to face him and held out the apple. He took it and took a bite. It was sweet and delicious, and he slowly chewed the fruit, savoring it. He took one more bite and handed it back. She finished the apple, dropping the core on the ground. With this little ritual, some type of relationship was established. Words weren't needed.

Julia looked Alex over curiously. She was at least a year older and much more mature than Alex. She knew the nature of the groups and that sooner or later, she would have to pick a partner-protector, or they would just subdue her and pass her around. Some things were inevitable down here. Several years before, she had been with the group boys when Brian and his friends took Alex on and saw what he did to them. She knew he was young and a loner, but she thought she might be able to mold him into something, a friend or maybe something more. His body never had that sour stink of the other boys, and he didn't get sick like they did. He went his own way, and she knew he was alone now. What she didn't know was how deep his mean streak went. He had no restrictions when attacked, so how would he deal with her? In a couple of years, maybe even now, she'd be powerless to stop him. She knew he was interested in her; he just didn't know why. They were still young, so they could be friends without the complications of sex.

Julia turned toward the door, turned to look at him, then started to walk outside. Alex followed silently.

Once outside, she pointed south and said, "Home," and began walking up the street. After a slight hesitation, Alex followed her. Julia went up to Second Street and turned right toward Elwood Avenue. Alex was confused; Julia was headed toward gang territory, and they both knew better than to go near them. She continued on and then turned left into an alley behind the old restaurant. Alex knew the alley was a dead end, but he followed her into it to see where she was headed. About halfway into the alley, she stopped. The back of the old building had a steel door that had been used for deliveries. It had a locking bar and padlock across it. Julia looked up and down the alley, then leaned over and lifted the bar and padlock up into the air. Apparently, it wasn't really attached to anything. She pushed on the steel door, and it opened inward. She disappeared inside.

Curious, Alex continued into the alley until he was at the doorway. He looked inside, but it was too dark—he could only see vague shapes of old furniture. He stepped inside and almost jumped because Julia was standing two feet from him at the corner of the door. She motioned him farther inside and closed the door behind him. He heard her drag a board across the door, probably blocking it from being opened from outside. He stood still, not knowing where to go next. He felt rather than heard her come up to his side. She took his hand and led him across the large restaurant floor between broken chairs and tables piled haphazardly. He could make out another doorway as they got closer to it, one of those swinging doors. This must be a kitchen, he thought. She pulled him through the door and let go of his hand. He stood there while she moved further into the kitchen. Suddenly, light flared, blinding him momentarily. When he could see again, he looked around in wonder.

To his right was an old gas range and a beat-up refrigerator. On his left were a long counter and a two-basin sink. What really surprised him was a bed built into the wall and, across from that, a small oval rug and an old easy chair in front of a door going somewhere. At the end of the room were another closed doorway and a chest of drawers. An old cat sat on the dresser, staring evilly at him. This was where she lived, he thought.

"Home?" he asked.

"Home," she replied, watching him examine the room.

"Look," she said, pointing to the closed door behind the easy chair. Alex turned and walked over to the door, opened it, and looked in. It was a bathroom with a toilet and a sink. Then he noticed the toilet had water in the bowl. *How could that be?* he wondered. He walked into the bathroom and looked at the sink. He turned the hot water faucet on, but nothing happened. Then he turned on the cold water, and water came out. Again he wondered, *How can that be?* No one had running water anymore. He stepped back out of the bathroom and turned to face her, confusion showing clearly on his face.

"How?" he said, holding his hands up in the air.

"Friend hook water, electric."

"Where's friend?" Alex asked.

"Gone." She turned away from him. The conversation was over.

Julia knew that Alex's mother had died; all the group kids knew. That meant that he, like she, was alone unless they wanted to live with the groups. Julia had always stayed close to the group kids but never stayed there overnight. They never asked her where she went, and she never volunteered the information. She just showed up each morning and spent the day with them, looking for whatever they could find or steal. But now, with Alex, life was going to change. He was her ticket out of the groups. She turned back to face him and walked closer to him. She looked into his eyes and said, "You, me, home." She pointed at him, then at herself, then around the room. Alex said nothing; he just looked at her.

"OK?" she said. He still said nothing, just looked at her. Then he turned toward the door without answering.

Chapter 7

That was the beginning of Julia and Alex. To Alex, there were so many new things to think about that he sometimes got confused. He'd never had a friend, not a real friend, and he didn't quite know how to deal with her. Because she seemed to know what they were supposed to do and how they were supposed to act, he followed her lead.

The first real test was when she asked him to go into the bathroom and wash. He thought about it and decided to do as she asked. He went into the bathroom and took off his clothes. Near the basin faucet were a rag and a small piece of soap. He got the rag wet and rubbed some soap into it. Then he scrubbed his neck and face, being careful not to get soap in his eyes. He soaped up the wet rag again and rubbed his head, washing his hair. He rinsed the soap out of the rag and rubbed his hair until most of the soap was gone. He soaped the rag again and continued washing his entire body. When he was done scrubbing, he rinsed the soap from the rag and washed his body with just water. When done, he used his old clothes as a towel.

It was warm in the building, but his skin tingled from the cold-water scrubbing. He picked up his dirty clothes and walked back into the main room. Julia was sitting on the bed and got off and walked over to him. She put out her hand to him, but he didn't know what she wanted. She said, "Clothes," and motioned for him to hand them to her. Maybe he was supposed to wear clothes in the room, but he really didn't want to put them back on because he was clean and it felt good. But he did as she asked and gave her the dirty clothes. She turned away and took them into the bathroom. When she came out, she had a man's shirt in her hand. She handed it to him and turned back to the bed. He unfolded the shirt and put it on. It was at least four sizes too large, but that didn't matter. It came down almost to his knees.

Dressed, he didn't know what to do next. Julia had climbed back on the bed and moved over to the far-left side. She pointed at the light switch and then the bed beside her. Alex turned the light off and climbed into bed beside her.

He woke before light. As soon as he moved, Julia's eyes popped open, staring at him. He didn't say anything but rolled to the edge and got out of bed. He went into the bathroom to relieve himself and remembered to flush the toilet. He saw his old clothes stacked on a box in the corner. They smelled clean now, so he took off the shirt and hung it on a nail. He put his old clothes on even though they were still damp, then his shoes. When he came back out, she was sitting up on the bed.

"Leaving," she said. It was a statement, not a question. He nodded yes and went out through the kitchen door. Julia came up behind him. Alex lifted the board out of the brackets that locked the door from the inside. He set the board against the wall and started to pull the door open. It was almost black in the dining room with little glints of gray light coming through the boarded-up windows. The cat ran by, lightly brushing his legs as it positioned itself to jump out the open door. Surprised, he jumped straight up and heard Julia make a little gurgle noise like a laugh underwater. He felt her put pressure on his shoulder, so he stood still.

"Wait," she said in a quiet voice. She slid a small metal panel open on the door. He could see her looking up and down the alley. She turned and nodded, and he opened the door, and he and the cat slipped out. He heard the door close and lock behind him. He pushed on the door to make sure it was locked, then melted back down the alley to Old Town.

Chapter 8

Alex didn't see Julia for two days. Each afternoon he went back to the alley and to her door, being careful not to be seen. He stood outside, hoping the observation panel would slide open and she would let him in. He didn't dare make noise for fear of being seen or heard, but each time, the panel and door stayed closed.

He had gifts for her. Alex had gone back to his old apartment after leaving Julia. He had grouped what clothes he had and got what was left of his mother's clothes and a pair of shoes, surprised that they were still there. He grabbed his old toothbrush but didn't have any toothpaste. Alex had decided to go through the other apartments in the building that were empty. He knew anything of trade value would have been removed long ago, but he was looking for things the group kids wouldn't care about. He found what he was looking for and went back to his room. He kept the knapsack ready with his clothes and goods inside.

Alex didn't know why he kept going back to Julia's lair. They had hardly spoken a word, but each had something the other needed. He liked being around her but wasn't really sure why. He had no clue why Julia had picked him out or what she intended. For her part, she didn't really know either. Some sense of hers had picked him for an upcoming role, and she was used to obeying her senses. She was also bothered that she kept picturing him standing naked, a man-child completely unabashed. She wondered what he would do if she stood in front of him like that. From his reaction to her, probably nothing. That was good, so why did she feel bad about it?

Julia kept Alex away for a few days because she wanted to know if that bond between them would stand up when they were apart and if he could be trusted. Their bond had nothing to do with affection, which was not a feeling practiced by the groups. They needed each other, and she probably needed him more than he needed her. She knew he had come back alone both days but wanted to wait a little while before letting him back in. Next time maybe she would sleep in the bed without holding her knife under the pillow.

Alex was up near the old theater when he saw Julia across the street. She was standing back near the ticket window, and for some reason, she seemed to be waiting for something. The first thing he noticed was that the spot she was waiting in had no back exit. The only way she could leave that area was the way she came in, and that wasn't like Julia—she always had a way out. Alex stepped back behind an old bus to watch her strange behavior. Out of the corner of his eye, he saw movement. Up the street, about half the block, were two of the older group boys. They were moving stealthily. Then it dawned on him that they were stalking her. He needed to warn her, so he picked up a piece of broken mirror and, using the sun, shined the reflection at her, hoping to get her attention. It worked. She turned her head toward him, and he stepped further away from the bus so she could see him. He motioned toward the two boys and pantomimed running away from the theater. She just looked at him, then turned her head toward the direction the boys were coming from. They were almost on her, and Alex, in panic, started to run across the street to her aid. Suddenly she burst out of the theater and ran straight at the two boys. That's when Alex noticed the stick in her hand. Before he could get to her, Julia had knocked both boys down and was beating them. She stopped when he ran up, turned to look at him, and then quietly walked away.

Chapter 9

The next day, Alex saw Julia and her group at the old railroad yard near the river. As usual, she stood a little distance from the boys. Two of the younger boys and one girl stood near her. The boys who had tried to attack her the day before gave her a wide berth. Alex could see the blue and purple bruises caused by her stick. It would just be a matter of time until they or other boys from the group went after her again. She might not be so lucky next time, but she was really good and really careful. Maybe she'd be OK.

Julia saw Alex cross the road down the tracks. She bobbed her head, hoping he'd see it as a signal to come by the alley later. He saw her head move but ignored her and kept going. He'd think about it later, but right now, Carmen had told him that a refrigerator delivery truck was broken down by the river, and that's where he was headed. If the groups or gangs got there first, he'd be out of luck.

He came around the old signal house and saw the truck. The driver had gotten too close to the ditch, and his wheels went off the shoulder and pulled him in. The truck hadn't tipped over, but it was on its side in the ditch near the old train tracks. The refrigerator was off, so everything in the back would spoil unless it was transferred quickly.

The driver was standing up on the street talking to someone on his cell phone as Alex sneaked down the ditch to the back of the truck. The doors had not sprung open, but he saw that there was no padlock on the latches. He got up to the doors and pulled the latch toward him. It screeched but not too loudly, so he kept pulling. The door was unlatched, but because the truck was on its side, Alex couldn't swing the doors open. He managed to lever one door open enough to wedge his body between it and the doorpost. He pulled himself up onto the bumper, losing a patch of skin on the doorjamb. He pushed the door open enough to get his head inside and then squeezed the rest of his body inside the truck.

The door closed quietly. It was pitch black inside, but Alex knew where the inside lights were because he'd seen refrigerator boxes before. He felt around the passenger side wall until he felt it near the door and pushed the button.

The dim battery light was enough to see the tumbled boxes. Quickly scanning the labels, he found one that said "NY STRIP." He didn't know what that meant, but it must be meat. The box was heavy, but he managed to get it from under the other cartons where he could open it. He used a nail from his jacket pocket to slice the packing tape.

Inside were dozens of single-wrapped steaks. He started putting the frozen steaks into his jacket through the ripped lining. They were heavy, and he might have to run, so he had to limit what he could take. Alex put nine of the strip steaks in his jacket and one package of frozen oven-ready rolls. That was about all he could grab quickly. He went to the back doors, clicking off the light. He was about to open the right-hand door when he heard the latch being opened. Voices started getting louder as they pulled the right door open.

Sunlight streamed into the back of the truck. Alex was pressed up against the left side, trying to stay out of sight. The driver stuck his head in but was concentrating on the boxes jumbled against the side of the truck. He never looked in the other direction, or Alex would have been spotted.

Alex could see the other man behind him. He would have to jump out of the truck, roll to his feet, and run as fast as he could. The problem was the drop from the back of the truck to the ground. He might break or sprain something when he jumped out, and then they'd catch him. Alex decided to launch himself at the second man, using him as a cushion for his fall.

The driver turned his back to the truck and started to talk to the other man. Alex moved to the open door and shot out, landing squarely on the shoulders of the driver who was facing away from him, knocking him into the astonished man standing in front of him. He rode them both to the ground and jumped up before they could gather their wits and grab him. He took off like a rocket, his jacket full of steaks flapping behind him.

Julia and her group watched Alex's escape go down. Shew was impressed. Alex was small, but he was fearless. He had taken out two full-grown men and was gone. She saw him standing naked in front of her again and cleared her throat to erase the image. Some of the boys grumbled that they should go after him, but unless four or five would do it, they wouldn't take him on. They let him go, Alex's prestige growing with the groups from the theft and the escape. Julia couldn't help but wonder if he was really as young as she thought.

Alex went straight back to his old apartment. When he was finished packing, he removed the brace from the inside of his door and unlocked it, opening it just a crack. The old hallway was quiet and deserted. He went into the hallway, locking the door behind him. The lock wouldn't keep someone serious from getting in, but that was the chance he had to take. Only two apartments had people living in them, and he quietly passed by those doors. The other empty apartments functioned as transient quarters for whoever was passing through or needed a place to do their drugs.

Outside, he looked cautiously in all directions and hurried down the sidewalk toward the old business district. He carried his bag of clothes in his left hand and his club in his right hand where anyone interested in him would see it. The steaks and rolls were stuffed into the clothes in the bag. He turned the corner on Fifth Street and saw shadows near a burned-out record store. He melted into an old stoop and watched the shadows for a while. Some group boys were holed up in there, cigarette smoke making little plumes in the air until the wind blew it away. He didn't know if Julia was with them, but he went back around the corner to avoid them. A block lower, he turned down Third Street and cautiously made his way toward Julia's alley.

Chapter 10

Alex stopped often, looking back to see if anyone was watching or following him. Before turning into the alley, he waited behind a pile of garbage, making sure he was alone. After fifteen minutes, he stood up and turned down the alley. When he got to the back door of the restaurant, he knocked quietly, scanning the area for anyone watching him. He could have waited until night, but the odds of being seen weren't much different. Alex heard the two-by-four being lifted down; Julia was home. The door opened quietly, and he saw her standing back in the shadows. He slipped inside, closing the door behind him. He replaced the two-by-four and turned around to face her, but she was gone.

Alex made his way across the old dining room, the gray light strong enough for him to avoid tripping on the broken chairs and tables. He went through the kitchen door, and the first thing he noticed was the sweet smell he knew was soap. She must have been washing in the bathroom. He was surprised she'd heard him knock.

He sat down in the easy chair, waiting for her to finish. He heard little noises coming from behind the closed door as he sat there patiently. About five minutes passed. Alex realized he was still wearing the homemade backpack. He wouldn't take off his jacket or the pack until she gave him the OK. This was her space and her rules.

Julia came out of the bathroom. She was rubbing her hair with a towel. He noticed the towel still had its original color and seemed to be clean. She must have a source of linens. Julia was wearing the man's shirt he had worn, buttoned up to her chin. It was easily four sizes too big, but he liked her in it. She went over to the dresser by the escape door. The same cat was sleeping on the top, but then Alex noticed it wasn't asleep—its yellow eyes were locked on him. She reached into the top drawer and took out a knot of colored material. She unrolled it, and the colored material became socks. She came over and sat on the bed, reaching down to put them on. He watched her, catching glimpses of a bare thigh. She paid no attention to him, but he felt embarrassed for some reason as if he had done something wrong. He turned his head back toward the cat while she finished dressing.

When she finished with the socks, Julia got off the bed and went into the bathroom to finish dressing. She came out dressed and went over to Alex. She put out her hand. For a minute, he didn't know what she meant, and then he realized she wanted his backpack. He slipped the rope off his shoulders and gave it to her. She turned and went over to the old commercial refrigerator and opened the door. He saw other wrapped items in it, and she put the contents of the pillowcase inside and gave his pack back to him. *Surely, it doesn't work*, he thought, looking at the old refrigerator. She came back over to him and put her hand out. He didn't have anything to give her, so he put his hand out too. She took his fingers in hers and pulled at him until he got up.

Julia thought it was time for the group kids to see them together. It might help protect her, she hoped. Of course, it could also backfire if they thought she was a way to get to him. This meant she was committed to building some kind of relationship with him. She'd have to give up the protection of the group boys, but it was time. Between the two of them, they could probably take care of themselves, at least for now.

Julia checked the alley and saw no one lurking. She hoped they could stay here; the restaurant was a real find, but it had weaknesses if there was ever a real attack. No place was really safe as long as they stayed in the lower end of town.

It was 2:00 PM, the weather warm and dirty as they made their way up to Fourth Street. Julia wanted to show Alex a place about eight blocks away that was good pickings for fruit. As they walked and dodged their way toward the higher streets, they both kept a lookout for groups or gangs that might be in the area. Generally, daytime was the quiet time since both parties liked to operate in the evening when they were harder to spot and the uptown customers were out looking to score. Alex kept an eye open for cops. Up here in the higher streets, two kids on the street were reason enough to get rousted by the police, thinking they were probably drug mules. The higher they went, the more the topography changed.

Now there was light traffic, and a few businesses were open as they moved farther from Old Town.

Alex was always nervous away from Old Town and tried to avoid coming here in daylight. Julia seemed to know where they were going, so he tried to ignore his misgivings and follow her. He was on high alert, ready to fight or run at a moment's notice. She turned down Laurel Street and then right, up a dirt alley behind the stores facing Fremont.

Garbage was piled in dumpsters and trash cans in the back. The smell of rotting meat and vegetables was strong. Stray dogs and cats took turns rummaging for the waste that dropped on the ground, and Alex had competed with them for leavings many times before.

Julia stopped at the back of a store. The screen door was closed, but they could see inside. It was some kind of farmers' market with tables filled with local produce. People were inside haggling over oranges and tomatoes. A mixture of English and Spanish was being spoken.

Julia went up to the door, but Alex went behind the dumpster, out of sight. She stood there until a woman in a stained apron came out and gave her something wrapped in newspaper. She smiled at the woman and turned away from the door. Worried about how exposed she was, Alex motioned her to come behind the dumpster. She looked at him and shook her head no, then turned and started to walk back out of the alley. She wasn't even trying not to be seen. Alex waited until she turned the corner, then slipped from hiding place to hiding place in pursuit. When he got to the corner of Laurel Street, she was nowhere in sight.

Alex made his way back to Julia's lair, taking pains not to be seen. He never caught up with her and hoped she would be there when he arrived. He turned down her alley and knocked on the metal door. Immediately, he heard the post being removed, and the door swung open. He ducked in, closing and locking it behind him. As usual, she was nowhere to be seen, so he went back to the kitchen door and went inside.

Julia was doing something with the fruit on the counter. She turned to look at him and motioned to the chair, so he walked over and sat down. The dresser cat watched him warily.

What do I do with him now? she thought, preparing the food. *He's too restless to sit there while I clean the fruit.* Then she had it; she'd send him to the basement to explore. He'd like that because then he'd know how to use the emergency escape.

She turned to face him. "Basement!" she said, pointing to the door by the dresser.

He looked confused. "Go there?" he asked.

She nodded yes.

He stood up and was looking for something. "Light?" he said, pointing to the candle on the sill.

"No," she said, "switch."

Alex nodded yes and walked to the door. Reaching in, he felt for the switch and flipped it on. He disappeared down the stairs.

The basement was large and tall enough to stand up in. Attached to the open beams were wires and pipes running in every direction. The block walls formed rooms with openings but no doors. An old furnace sat in one of the walled rooms. Iron pipes, probably old steam pipes, ran from the rusted-out furnace boiler up through the walls and ceiling to where radiators had been upstairs. The pipes and boiler were rusted badly, probably from water being left in them for years.

Alex noticed what looked like a scuffed path worn across the broken concrete floor. He followed it through two more of the block-walled rooms with nothing in them but pipes and wires. At the far end of the last room, he saw another door. It looked to be in fair condition and had the same hooks, bolt, and two-by-four post locking it shut.

Alex went over to it. He pulled out the bolt and removed the post. He unlocked the door handle and turned it to the right. The door opened quietly, so Julia had been oiling the hinges. The door led into another basement, probably the building next door. This basement was one big room, and the foundation and walls were crumbling stone. It looked older than Julia's basement, and he could barely tell that another door was at the far end of the room. There were no lights in this building. Alex could only see by the light from her basement, but it was enough for him to get to the other door.

Like her other doors, this one was secured with the post. He removed it and unlocked the door handle. It swung inward quietly, obviously maintained by someone. This time, however, the door opened outward onto an outside path flanked on each side by block walls. There was no roof, but it was completely covered over by oleander bushes grown together to form a crown. He had about four feet of room from the bottom of the path to the top of the block walls, then another foot to the branches of the oleanders. The path had a slow incline, probably bringing it up to a street level at the end of the walls. It was a completely hidden walkway.

Alex cautiously went up the path. It was lighter outside, and he could see better. After about twenty feet, the path ended with an old garbage bin blocking the path entrance. He couldn't figure out why it would dead-end unless this wasn't her escape route. The bin completely blocked the path, but when he pushed on it, it rolled easily to the left. A secret entrance and exit. He didn't want to push the big trash bin out of the way in case someone was watching, so he turned around and went back inside the building. When he closed and locked the door, he had to stand there until his eyes got accustomed to the dim light. Alex headed back to Julia's basement. All the time he was down there, he could feel hundreds of little eyes watching him, but the rats stayed away.

Back in her kitchen, Julia waited for Alex to return. She felt it was time to tell him some of her plan. Once he saw the escape path, he should feel more secure in her building. That was good because her plan included him moving in with her. She heard scraping noises and knew Alex was coming back. The cat was up and alert, nervous about the basement noises and ready to run. She reassured him, and he sat down, still watching the basement door and ready to disappear. Alex came into the kitchen, and the cat, still watching him intently, settled down.

"Alex," she said, pointing to the chair. Julia was still unused to having conversations with anyone and reverted to single syllables automatically. He nodded and crossed the room, sitting in one of the chairs. She took a deep breath, went over to Alex, and kneeled down in front of him.

"Alex," she said softly, "I want you to move in here with me. I know you're alone, and so am I, and we can help each other. I won't be a burden, and I think we can be friends."

Julia stopped talking. Alex just looked at her, not saying anything. *Oh god*, she thought, *he's going to say no*. He just stared at her, not saying anything. She was getting nervous.

"Say something." It sounded like an order, and she didn't mean to say it like that. She was nervous, and that made her angry. This was unfamiliar territory. Alex shook his head and then said yes.

CHAPTER 11

In the basement, Julia showed Alex the gas and water connections. Someone had run black pipe through the two basements to an old city gas meter station on Second Street. The city must have missed this connection. They had pulled the meter and plugged it off, but the black pipe was connected to where the plug had been installed, and the city must have forgotten to shut the supply down to the old station. Same with the water connection. An old galvanized water pipe ran beside the gas pipe and connected to where the old water meter used to be attached to the pipe coming through the stone foundation. It was another missed connection, capped off where the water meter had been. But the water still flowed from the main. The galvanized pipe was connected with a galvanized tee, with one end plugged off. Alex still didn't know how she had electricity, but he'd find out later.

They went back upstairs to the kitchen. Julia went to the old refrigerator and took out the pillowcase with the steaks and rolls. Alex watched her curiously. She took out two wrapped steaks and two rolls and put the rest back. Putting the food on the steel prep table, she took out a tomato and onion and began slicing them up. The meat was partially frozen still, but the rolls had thawed out. Julia got out an old, battered aluminum pan and put the steaks, sliced tomatoes, and onion in it. She took the rolls and put them on a flat cookie sheet. Then she went to the old stove and lit a top burner with a match, opened the oven and lit the inside burner. She put the frying pan on the stovetop and got a jar of murky liquid out of the refrigerator. It was too thick to pour, so she spooned some into the pan, then put the jar back.

Good smells were already coming from the food. Alex realized he hadn't eaten since the day before, and his stomach started complaining. He was used to going without meals, but the cooking smells were driving him crazy. He was afraid someone would smell the food outside, but she didn't seem concerned. The cookie sheet with the rolls went into the oven. He sat in the chair, watching her work. He was having mixed feelings about moving in. He didn't want to be responsible for anyone, but in her defense, she wouldn't need much from him. She had a great lair, and he knew between them, food wouldn't be an issue.

What really bothered him was how confused he got around her. He wasn't used to anyone making decisions for him, and she tended to jump in and do what she felt was best. That might not be what he wanted, and they'd have to work out some kind of arrangement. But what bothered him most was that she affected him physically, and that was completely new to him. He was naive when it came to men and women and physical relationships. He was twelve now and considered mature by group standards, but in reality, he had no clue how to deal with these new feelings. Not growing up with a group, he'd had little or no interaction with females except his mother, and he didn't want to look stupid or do or say something wrong to her.

Julia moved the food off of the stove onto the prep table. She turned off the burner and oven, then used an old rag to grab the cookie sheet from the oven. No one had cooked for Alex since his mom died. He was impressed, and he got up to help.

"Wash," she said, pointing to the bathroom. He did as he was told and then came back.

"Help?" he asked, looking for plates and silverware. Julia pointed to an old cupboard that had a curtain over it. He went to the cupboard, and a hodgepodge of cups and dishes were stacked inside. Silverware was also piled on one side. He grabbed two plates, cups, forks, and knives and came back. She had no dining room, so he set them on the prep table.

Julia took a fork and put one steak on each of the plates. Then she spooned the vegetables on top and placed two rolls with each. She picked up her plate and a cup and headed to the throw rug on the floor. Alex followed suit, bringing her silverware. He took their cups into the bathroom and filled them with water from the tap. When he got back, Julia was already chewing with relish.

Alex forked the steak up to his mouth and tore off a piece of meat. The flavor almost hurt; it was so good. He forked some vegetables and chewed them with the meat. Both of them concentrated on the food, not talking. In the groups on the street, you ate what you could as fast as you could. Both attacked their food with gusto; talking could wait.

Julia was done first and let out a big sigh of satisfaction. Alex wasn't far behind. She waited for him to finish before saying anything.

"You liked it," she said. It was a statement, not a question.

"That was so good," he said, rubbing his stomach. He smiled at her, and she smiled back, lighting the room.

She got up and said, "Come, bring the dishes." He did as she asked, and they washed them together in the bathroom sink.

"I could fix the kitchen sink to work," he said.

She smiled at him again. They dried the dishes and silverware with a clean rag hanging above the toilet. She gathered them and stacked them back in the cupboard. "We never leave dirty dishes," she said.

Alex grew up with the rats; he already knew that rule. The cat had watched them eat, but neither he nor Julia offered him scraps, and he didn't seem to expect it. People's food was for people, not animals. The cat had lots of food living in the basement.

Julia came into the little living area. Alex was sitting in the easy chair, and when she sat down on the rug, she motioned him to join her. She looked at him without speaking. Alex started getting nervous, not used to close scrutiny from anyone, especially a girl.

"Can you read," she asked.

"Yes," Alex said, "Spanish and English, but I don't spell good."

"I'll help you learn," she said.

"Why?" Alex asked curiously.

"You need to read and write good in other places," she said.

Alex didn't know what "other places" meant, so he just nodded yes to please her.

Julia yawned suddenly and stretched.

"Clean up and sleep," she said, getting up and heading for the bathroom. She was giving him orders again, and he wasn't sure he liked it. He waited a few minutes and got up, joining her in the bathroom. She had the sink filled with cold water and was using the piece of soap and rag to wash her face and arms.

"Hand me the shirt," she said, pointing behind her. He turned and took it off the hook. It was the man's large shirt both of them had worn before. She unconsciously unbuttoned her jeans, letting them fall down around her ankles. She used the soapy rag to wash her bottom and between her legs. She paid no attention to Alex, who tried not to watch her. Julia unbuttoned her shirt and removed it, completely naked now. Using a different rag, she got it wet and soapy, washing her underarms, neck, and breasts. Her breasts were larger than he had thought, and the cold water made her nipples stand out. She had a tiny waist and flat stomach, and the muscles of her back rippled as she washed. Her skin was smooth without the sores most of the group kids had.

Julia toweled off with another of the hanging rags and then slipped the large shirt over her head without unbuttoning it. She turned to face him, a strange expression on her face, then bent down to untie his shoes.

She moved behind him so he could wash next, but she didn't leave. He followed her routine, removing his shoes and socks, then his pants. Like her, he soaped up with the wet rag she had used for her bottom and washed his butt and between his legs. Rinsing it, he soaped the rag and washed his legs and feet. The cold water felt good because the kitchen was still warm from cooking. He took off his shirt and was now naked. He rinsed out the rag and put it on the sink. He got the rag she'd used on her face and used it to scrub his neck and face. He rinsed the rag off and used it to wash his hair without the soap.

He'd forgotten she was even there until she put her hand on his shoulder and gave him another of the large shirts. He unbuttoned the two top buttons and slid the shirt over his head. Then he went out into the kitchen carrying his dirty clothes and dropped them on one of the old chairs. Julia came out of the bathroom and went to pick up his dirty clothes, but he asked for his pants back. Alex took out the three marbles and gave the pants back to her. She looked at him curiously, then took the clothes into the bathroom and came back out. Then she went over to the kitchen sink with the two washrags they'd used and hung them up, one on each side of the sink.

"Remember, the blue one is for your bottom and feet," she told him.

Julia crossed over to the bed. It was dark outside. They had full bellies, and he was starting to get sleepy. She climbed up on the bed and moved over near the wall. He climbed in after her, leaving the light on. Julia took a large thin book down from the shelf above her head.

"Alex, do you ever read books?" she asked him. He noticed that they were talking in sentences, not just single words, and that was fine with him. *It probably means we're friends*, he thought, and that pleased him.

"Sometimes, when I find one, I read it. I read really slow, and I can't always figure out what they're talking about. It takes me a long time to read them, and I can only do it while it's still light. If it has pictures, that helps."

She showed him the book she was holding. He read the title, *A Tourist Guide to El Paso, Texas.*

"This book tells people what interesting places are in El Paso," she said.

Alex laughed. "Yeah, like Old Town and the safe zone. Ha ha ha."

"No, silly, it talks about nice places like Chamizal Memorial National Park where they have shown every week about the Mexican and American culture or the zoo. Wouldn't it be great to see some of those things?" She looked at Alex expectantly.

"Julia, those things are uptown, and we'll never go there, so there's no reason to even think about them." He rolled onto his left side, facing away from her.

She looked at his back for a few seconds. "You're wrong," she said to him and settled down to look at the book.

Alex didn't answer, but he thought, *Why even think about things like that?* He clutched the marbles tighter. He was angry with her for making him think about it.

Chapter 12

In the morning, Alex felt Julia climbing over him to get out of bed. The light was still on from the night before.

"Are you hungry?" she asked.

"No, I don't usually eat anything for breakfast," he replied.

"Me either," she said, "but let's go up to Laurel Street and see if we can get some food for later."

"OK," he said, "but let's check with Hector to see if anything is going on before we go there. Do you know him?"

"Is he the Mexican boy with the shriveled arm?" Julia asked.

"Yeah," Alex said. "Hector usually runs with the group from Sixth Street, but he knows what the other groups and the gangs are up to. We should know that before we go near their turf."

"Smart," she said.

Alex felt a glow of pride. They took turns dressing in the bathroom this time. His socks were dry, and he put them back on. He noticed that Julia did not put on her beanie, and her dark hair glistened. She was also wearing a top that fit tighter than the ones she usually wore, and he wondered about that. He was used to seeing her in baggy shirts and big pants cinched at her waist. Her hair was always covered.

They checked the alley, then went out the door and locked it. She started skittering, and he flitted from shelter to shelter like her. He didn't want any of the gang members to see them, and her alley was too close to them to make him comfortable. They made it up to Sixth Street and Center Street, where the old YMCA had burned years ago. This was where Hector's group usually hung out. They stopped on the corner behind a concrete column and watched the building. Now and then, shadows moved inside the dim building. Alex didn't see any lookouts, which was surprising.

"Stay here and let me go in. I'll call you when it's OK."

Julia nodded yes. He stepped out into the street where he could be seen. You never sneak up on a group; they could react badly.

"Alex, who is that with you behind the column?" a voice called out from inside the building.

They must have lookouts hidden somewhere, he thought.

"It's Julia from Fourth Street. She's with me."

There was a long pause, then the voice said, "Have her come out into the street." Julia heard this and came out from behind the column to stand next to him. More silence.

"OK, you can come in but leave your club there in the street. Is she armed?"

Julia answered, "No."

Alex dropped his club, and they crossed the street. As he got closer, he saw about a dozen kids in the building. Most of them had some kind of weapon in their hands and moved back, giving them room to move if there was trouble. This was pretty standard with the groups. Alex went in first, Julia right behind him. Inside, he looked around for Hector and saw him farther back in the building. No one said anything to them.

They moved farther back toward Hector.

"Hola, Hector, como se dice," he said.

Hector grinned. "Que?"

"We need to know what the gangs and groups are doing around Laurel Street," Alex told him.

"We?" It was a statement, not a question.

Alex didn't answer.

"Bloods are selling drugs on Hilltop, so don't go that way. No groups up there."

"Bien," Alex said. Then he turned to Julia. "We'd better go."

They turned to leave, but Randy, the group leader, was standing in their way to the door. "Leave her here," he said, eying Julia. "She's group, not a loner, and she can stay with us."

Alex felt rather than saw Julia move back to give her fighting room.

"No," Alex said, preparing to attack.

Hector yelled, "Let them go, Randy! You know what's gonna happen if you try to stop Alex, and you won't be the only one. She's just as mean as he is."

The other kids didn't know what to do, and they waited to follow Randy's lead. Alex figured he would take Randy, then at least five more. Julia was worth about the same. Between them, they'd take out all the older kids quickly, girls and boys.

Randy didn't want to lose face in front of his group. He was bigger than Alex and was used to bullying the other kids. He knew Alex was a good fighter, but he figured he was better. The girl he ignored.

"You don't give the orders here. If I say—" He never finished his sentence. Julia was ready, but Alex moved so fast, she was still standing there when Randy went down. The other kids hung back. The ferocity of Alex's attack and Randy's scream when Alex broke his arm unnerved them. He'd hit Randy in the face with three quick jabs and rode him to the ground. Then he purposely broke Randy's right arm using his knee as a fulcrum. The blood from his nose and the scream and sound of the bone snapping took the fight out of the other kids. Alex was back on his feet, facing the other kids, holding Randy's club, but no one moved.

"Leave, Alex! We won't stop you," Hector yelled over Randy's cries. Alex and Julia headed for the door, keeping a watch on the other kids. No one tried to stop them.

They left the area quickly, sacrificing stealth to put distance between them and the group.

Four blocks away, they stepped into a deserted storefront.

Julia put her hand on his shoulder and said, "Thank you, Alex." He looked at her and was embarrassed to see that her eyes were moist.

"OK," he said, smiling but not sure why it was a big deal. He didn't realize that she had always stood up for herself and never had anyone fight for her. Alex turned back to the street.

"If you want to go to Laurel Street, we should move now."

"Yes," she said, and they were on their way to the alley behind the market.

They put away the vegetables from the market. It was late afternoon, and they agreed to wait for dinner to eat. Alex waited with anticipation, remembering last night's meal. He'd get Julia to show him how to fix the food. Alex left her in the kitchen while he explored the first floor of the old restaurant while there was still some light.

Chapter 13

The dining room was piled with old tables and chairs, mostly broken or with bent legs. He thought maybe he could make an eating area near their kitchen so that they didn't have to eat on the floor. He found a small pedestal table that was in fair condition. If he could fix the tabletop so it didn't wobble, it would work fine. Finding two chairs that were still good was harder. He went back to the kitchen and asked her if she had a hammer. He figured she did with all the nails in the walls. Julia got it for him, and he left. She didn't ask him what he needed it for.

Alex pried nails out of the walls to use to fix the tabletop. The table was metal, but it had a wooden block between the pedestal base and tabletop. He pounded the nails through the thin steel top into the block, and it held it steady. The chairs took a little more work, but when he finished, he had two usable chairs. There were several folding privacy screens over by the public bathroom. They were six feet wide and about five feet tall in three sections. Some kind of mountain scene was painted on them, but they were so dirty that Alex couldn't tell what they were supposed to be.

He carried them over near the kitchen door and stacked three screens against the wall. Alex went back into the kitchen area and got a broom. He came back out and began sweeping an eight-foot area clean just to the right of the kitchen door. Once that was done, he dragged the table into the center of the clean spot, then put the two chairs up to the table. He set up the three screens, making a three-sided box. He sat down on one of the chairs. *Not bad*, he thought, then realized he would have to wash at least one side of the screens.

He heard Julia moving around the kitchen. He wanted this to be a surprise, so he quickly got up and went inside.

"What are you doing?" she asked, watching him put the broom back.

"Don't go out there," he answered, pointing to the kitchen door. She was curious but did as he said. *He's probably cleaning up some dead animal*, she thought, having removed stray cats and dogs that had died in the room. She didn't think much of it.

Around five o'clock, Julia went into the bathroom to start her evening clean-up. Alex was getting used to the routine. Still unsure if he was supposed to come in or wait, he sat in the chair. Julia opened the curtain and said, "Aren't you going to wash?"

I guess I'm going in, he thought, getting up from the chair. It went pretty much like the night before. Julia washed first, using the blue rag for her bottom and the white rag for her face. Like before, she undid her shoes first, sliding them and her socks off. Then she unbuttoned her pants and let them drop. She washed her bottom, feet, and between her legs with the blue rag. Then she rinsed it out and hung it on the left nail. She used the white rag and soap to wash her neck, arms, and breasts. Alex liked the way her butt was rounded instead of all angles like his. Her body was all curves, very different from his.

She probably thinks I'm really ugly, he mused.

Her skin was pale because it was usually covered up to her chin. Her face and arms had turned a light brown from the sun, unlike his much darker skin. Alex really enjoyed looking at her.

Julia knew Alex was looking at her, although she pretended she didn't. She wasn't embarrassed to be naked in front of him; it seemed harmless and natural. If he had tried to touch her, well, that would have been different, but she knew looking at her made him happy. Looking at him naked pleased her also. There was nothing wrong with that. Julia turned around to face him. She saw him stare at her breasts, then lower down. She stood there like in an inspection until he looked up at her. She smiled and took the shirt off the wall, slipping it over her head.

Alex felt embarrassed but didn't know why. She had turned so he could look at her, so it must be OK, but he still felt like he'd done something wrong. To make matters worse, looking at her like that had gotten him excited. How was he going to get undressed in front of her like that? He supposed this was normal, but he was afraid she'd be offended. He didn't know what to do; maybe she'd leave. This time he started washing by taking his shirt off. He could smell a slight odor of sweat, and even that embarrassed him. Jeez, it was getting so complicated being around her.

He used the white rag to scrub his face, neck, and arms. He wasn't going to wash his hair tonight, so he finished up. Like last night, Julia bent down and untied his shoes. This embarrassed him even more because he was afraid his feet smelled bad. One of the reasons he never slept with the group was the odor of unwashed bodies and stinking feet. She didn't make any sign that his feet smelled, but tonight, he was going to wash his socks with soap and hang them up to dry. He bent down and took his shoes off, then his socks.

Now, what do I do? he thought. His body was still excited. With a sigh, Alex unbuttoned his pants and let them drop, but they hung there. He was so embarrassed. He pulled his pants off the erection and let them fall. Alex never looked to see if she was watching and hoped she'd missed the whole thing. He kept his back to her as he washed his lower half. When he finished, he was still erect. He asked her to hand him the shirt and reached back without turning. Nothing happened. He turned his head, and she was standing there with the shirt in her hand.

"Turn around and face me," she said in a soft voice. He did as she said, almost shaking. He was so embarrassed and nervous. She looked at his body like he had looked at hers. She stared at his penis for a long time. Then she hung the shirt on it and turned to go into the kitchen. He was so shocked he just stood there like a clothesline. Finally, he got it together and slid the shirt over his head. Alex washed his socks with the soap, rinsed them, and hung them up to dry.

In the kitchen, Julia was getting the food out of the refrigerator as if nothing had happened. Alex thought about it and realized nothing had happened. It was all quite natural. He started feeling better about it.

"Show me how you fixed the meat," he said.

Julia pointed at the cutting board leaning against the wall near the prep table. "Get that. I'll show you how to cut everything up."

Alex grabbed the cutting board and put it on the prep table. He gathered the vegetables she got out and put them by the cutting board.

"Take out a zucchini, an onion, and a tomato. You're going to cut them up."

"What's a zucchini?" he asked, looking at the vegetables in the bag.

"The long green thing."

Alex saw two of them in the bag and took one out. "This?"

"Yes," she said, "you need to take the skin off first." She handed him an old paring knife with half the handle missing, and he started whittling on it.

"Try to leave some of the vegetable." She laughed as he cut chunks out of the squash. He slowed down and was able to leave most of the squash intact.

Proud of himself, he said, "Next?"

"You need to slice up the onion and tomato into small pieces."

She came over and showed him how to crosscut the onion, then cut it into small pieces. He did as she showed him, then cut up the tomato the same way. Finished with the vegetables, he went over to the stove, and she pulled out the old aluminum frying pan. "You have to use some kind of grease, or it will stick and burn."

She got the jar from the refrigerator. Like the night before, she spooned out some of the gray goo and put it in the pan.

"This is how you light it."

She got the butane lighter down and turned on the gas to the front burner. With a whomp, the burner lit. Julia put the frying pan with the grease on the burner, and it immediately started to melt. *It smells like bacon*, he thought. *Must be where she got the grease.*

"Bring the cutting board over with the vegetables."

Alex did as asked, pushing the vegetables into the bubbling grease. The aroma was wonderful.

"Keep stirring this while I get the meat."

Julia went back to the refrigerator and got out two more of the wrapped steaks. Alex's stomach was growling so loud Julia heard it. She smiled.

"It'll be ready soon. Can you get us two plates and cups?"

Alex went to the curtained cupboard and got them down. He saw the old kerosene lantern on the shelf and saw that it had some oil still in it. Julia was busy cooking, so he grabbed the lantern and the plates and went out the kitchen door. He put the plates on the table he'd set up and the lantern in the middle. Alex went back into the kitchen; Julia hadn't noticed him leaving. He picked up the lighter and went back into the dining room. Lighting the lantern, he turned the wick down until it stopped smoking, leaving a nice yellow glow in the little enclosure.

When he came back in, Julia saw him. "Everything OK?" she asked, probably thinking he was checking the alley.

"Yes," he said, gathering up the two cups and heading into the bathroom to fill them up. She had put one knife and two forks by the cups. Alex figured they would share the knife to cut the meat.

"About ready?" he asked.

Thinking he was just hungry, she said, "Only another minute," and smiled to herself. He slipped out the door with the cups and silverware, and she didn't notice. Alex was back in the kitchen, standing behind her while she finished the meat.

"Get the plates, and I'll dish it up," she said.

He'd forgotten about that, and the plates were outside on the table. He looked around and saw an old, cracked serving platter.

"Let's just put it all on the platter instead." She picked the platter off the shelf. She frowned for a minute, then shrugged. "You're doing the dishes." She scooped the food from the pan onto the platter and turned off the burner. When Julia turned around, she didn't see the plates or cups. "Where is everything?" she asked him.

Balancing the platter with one hand, he took her hand and said, "Close your eyes till I tell you to open them."

Confused, she started to object.

"Please, just do as I asked."

She looked at him, sighed, and closed her eyes. He led her out of the kitchen door, telling her to keep her eyes closed. He led her over to the little enclosure and put the platter on the table.

"OK, you can open them now."

Julia opened her eyes and gasped. The tiny little room was beautiful. He had washed the partitions, and snow-covered mountains looked out at them. The table was clean and shiny.

"It's so beautiful," she said to him, her eyes getting moist again. "No one has ever done anything like this for me before. Thank you." She didn't let go of his hand. She just stood there with her moist eyes melting him.

Uncomfortable again, Alex cleared his throat and said, "OK, well, let's eat." She finally let his hand go and sat down across from him. The lantern made the little room look good, he thought, but it was Julia that took his breath away.

Alex was now thirteen and had no experience with girls. What he knew about the other sex was what little he'd read and the conversations of the group boys. Most of that information was about sex; half of it was inaccurate, and it did nothing to educate him about emotions. He was very confused. Alex didn't know what to call their relationship, but he knew they had one. He'd do anything to protect her, and she would do the same for him. Somehow, they'd both decided that they were a couple without even talking about it. He still didn't think much about the sex part. He really didn't want to think about that; it was too unfamiliar. He had no idea how to make love to a girl and had no reason to think she was interested in this anyway. Seeing each other naked didn't really mean anything, nor did sleeping in the same bed. This was common in the groups. Alex figured he'd just botch it up anyway or upset her so much she'd leave. He'd rather not do anything to ruin what they were now, and he had other things to worry about, like survival. He did dream about touching her some nights, but he kept that to himself.

    For her part, Julia had made the decision about them before Alex did. She was more mature, not just because she was older but because she was a girl and had to learn about boys to protect herself. She was smart enough to know that as strong and fierce as he was, inside Alex was still a little boy, and she would have to lead him along. Not that she knew much about how to do that, but she knew her body, and she knew what she felt when she looked at him. Last night seeing him aroused almost made her reach for him, and that really scared her. Somehow, she sensed that it would have been a mistake. She'd better figure out how to handle this before it got out of hand. Fighting Randy for her was great, and she really appreciated his protection, but the little dining room, he shouldn't have done that. She knew he was trying to please her, but he had no idea how much that had meant to her. She was scared.

Chapter 14

They finished the dinner, and Alex thought it was even better than the night before. He knew that when the steaks ran out, they'd be back to whatever they could scrounge, and that was OK, but he'd had really liked this treat. He was happy that Julia liked his little surprise, but he didn't think it was that big of a deal. He got up and started collecting their dishes, and she followed suit. They washed the dishes in the bathroom, and although it was supposed to be his job, Julia helped. They talked about Hector's group and what had happened that day. It wasn't really a surprise, and Alex said she should probably keep her beanie on and dress down as much as possible so that she didn't draw too much attention. Julia took that as a compliment and said she would. He didn't say it, but he was really afraid someone from the gangs would notice her, and that would be a lot harder to deal with. Alex had no doubt that he would go up against the gangs for her, but he was under no illusion that it would end well for him—or for her.

After the dishes were done, they did the wash-up ritual. Alex was relieved that he didn't embarrass himself. Julia asked him if he would help her wash her hair. She unbuttoned her shirt enough to fold the collar inside and put her head under the faucet, getting her hair wet. She asked Alex to take the piece of soap and lather up her hair, and he did as she asked. It was thicker and softer than he thought. When she was done, she rinsed the soap out and used the towel folded on the toilet to dry it. She hung the towel on one of the nails to dry. She brushed her teeth and put the toothbrush back in the water glass by the sink. "Put your toothbrush in the glass when you're done," she said, turning and leaving the bathroom. Alex got the toothbrush out of his pack and saw the soap pieces and his mom's clothes still in it. He washed his teeth just using water, then put the toothbrush into the glass. *She's training me*, he thought and picked up the cloth backpack and left the bathroom.

Back in the kitchen area, Julia was already in bed. She had her book about El Paso and was thumbing through the pages. He walked over and showed her what he'd brought from his mom's apartment. She was pleased with the soap, he could tell. She'd try the clothes and shoes on later. Julia patted the bed beside her, and he climbed in.

"Look at this building," Julia said, pointing to a tall building with hundreds of glass windows.

"Wouldn't it be fun to see it?"

Alex wasn't sure. It was just a building in a part of town they couldn't go to, but he said yes just to make her happy. She smiled at him and put the book away. He got out of bed, turned the light out, and climbed back in. They settled down, and he lay there, not ready for sleep. He wanted to think about today. In the dark room, he could hear the cat getting ready for his nightly hunt for food. He felt the bed move, and suddenly, cold feet touched his thigh.

"Hey," he said, "your feet are freezing."

She snickered and pushed them under his legs.

"Warm them up, please," she said, and he could hear the laughter in her voice. Secretly, he liked her touch, but her feet really were cold.

"OK, but my turn next time."

They settled down to sleep; Julia curled up with her back to him and her feet under his legs. *If I were a cat, I'd purr*, she thought as she closed her eyes. She couldn't see Alex smiling in the dark.

Chapter 15

Alex was up first. He used the toilet and washed his teeth and face. Coming out, he saw Julia sitting up in bed. *Gosh, she's pretty*, he thought. Her clean hair was going in several directions, but she looked great to him.

She said, "Hi," and got out of bed and went into the bathroom. When she came out, she was wearing pants and a shirt at least three sizes too big, and her hair was completely covered with the beanie.

But I know what she really looks like, he thought to himself, smiling.

"What's so funny?" she said.

"Nothing, just feel good."

"I think I'll go to my group today and see what they're doing," Julia told him.

"Are you sure that's a good idea?" he said, thinking of the two boys she had fought with.

"I'll be fine. Nobody's going to bother me." She didn't say because they're afraid of you, but she knew it. "What are you going to do?"

Alex thought for a minute, then said, "If I can find the tools, I'd like to run water to the kitchen."

"You know how to do that?" she said, surprised.

"Yeah, I think so. My mom and I used to work on our plumbing all the time. Do you know if there are any tools around here?"

"Maybe in the janitor's closet in the basement. I'm not sure what's in there except rats."

"OK, I'll look there," he said.

"I should be back in a couple of hours," Julia said as she headed into the dining room. Alex walked out behind her to lock the door when she went outside. He didn't put the post back so she could unlock it and come in if he was downstairs. He went back into the kitchen and down into the basement, turning on the light.

Like before, the sound of scurrying feet was easily heard. He looked around and saw the old metal cabinet by the wall. Alex walked over and quickly opened the door, standing back in case any furry friends wanted out, but there were no rats inside. *Probably the smell of the oil kept them out*, he thought. Someone had stored kerosene or diesel oil in a coffee can, and it had spilled long ago, but the smell was still there. He saw a few hand tools, mostly in poor condition. There was an old pipe wrench that used a chain instead of jaws to clamp the pipes and a hacksaw with no blade. Alex grabbed both tools and looked through the other shelves. There was an old pair of channel-lock pliers with a broken handle, and he took that also. Nothing else was usable.

Alex went back upstairs with his find. He went over to the sink and looked underneath. The sink was a double-basin sink, and the drains were hooked together and connected to a pipe that disappeared through the wall. The sink drain was rusted through where it connected to the wall. The water supply lines were still there and didn't look too bad. Each had its own shutoff valve, and using the pliers, he opened them, not really expecting anything to happen.

He was right—nothing came out, but at least the valves didn't break off. He went back downstairs to try to find out where the pipes connected to the water supply. He saw the two copper lines from the sink where they came out of the kitchen into the basement and then connected to the galvanized supply lines. He followed the two supply lines, and one was connected to a tee that was hooked into the old hot water heater. The heater had rusted years before, and there was no water going to it. Alex was only interested in the cold-water supply anyway. He followed that line to the far wall. Julia had shown him where they had brought the water in for the bathroom. The pipe from the kitchen ran near the supply line, and it had a fitting connecting it to another pipe. It would be simple enough to disconnect the old line at the union thing and tee it into the supply line with a short piece of pipe. Simple—that is, if you had the tools and parts. Both pipes were three-quarter galvanized. He'd have to cut the old pipe and connect it to the fitting coming into the building. He knew who would have the parts he needed, but the price might be too high.

Chapter 16

Alex estimated the length of the pipe he would need and went back upstairs and sat down to think about it. He needed two elbow things and a fitting called a tee and then a three-foot section of pipe as long as the old fittings weren't too rusted to reuse.

With a sigh, Alex emptied his backpack out on the bed and slung it over one shoulder. He went out the kitchen door to the street door, looking through the panel first to make sure the area was clear. Alex locked the door behind him and went back out the alley, but instead of turning left toward the projects, he turned right on Laurel toward midtown. Alex was headed into Blood territory, and he walked in the center of the old street so the scouts would see him coming.

Five blocks up the street, the first signs of traffic showed up, and the farther he went, the more cars were on the street. This was where the city dwellers came to buy their drugs. He'd already gone by two Bloods hanging out in doorways, so the word would have gone out already. A group boy was on their turf. He knew it wouldn't be long until they stopped him. Sure enough, he saw three Bloods in the street on the next block. They'd know that if he kept coming, he must have business or a death wish. The group boys traded with the gangs sometimes, but they rarely had anything the Bloods really wanted, and you never knew if they'd just knife you without asking why you were there. Alex was taking the chance that they would ask first.

As he got nearer to the Blood stronghold, he thought he recognized one of the gang members from the warehouse. He stopped about ten feet away from them, waiting for instructions. He kept his hands in plain sight so they'd know he had no weapons. The Blood he thought he recognized walked toward him. He had a clasp knife in his left hand, but it wasn't open; that was a good sign. When he was three feet from Alex, he spoke.

"You, Alex." It wasn't a question.

"Yes," Alex said, never taking his eyes off the Blood.

"Heard 'bout what you did to Randy down on Sixth Street. Think that'd work with me?" He smiled coldly at Alex, showing missing teeth.

"No," Alex said, "I'm here with need." That meant he was there to trade, not fight.

"You got nothin' we need, nothin' we want." He looked disdainfully at Alex.

"I have service," Alex said, and the Blood blinked.

The Blood turned and walked back to his friends. They spoke for a minute, then the Blood turned back to him and said, "Come on." He turned back, and the three started walking up the street. Alex followed about five feet behind, just close enough so that the other Bloods saw he was with them.

Anson was boss today, just like almost every other day. He was the war chief for the Bloods and was only happy when they were fighting one of the other gangs or the police. He was vicious and smart, and that had kept him near the top of the food chain for two years, which was a lifetime for a gang member. He saw Brian and the two other Bloods come in with the group boy following. Anson didn't know the kid, but if he made it this far, he must have something the Bloods wanted. Brian was looking for Luke, the current leader of the Bloods, but Luke was out on the street, taking care of business. They'd have to talk to him instead. Brian was told Luke was out, so he turned and headed toward Anson. "At least this is something different," he thought, eying the kid.

"Anson, we got Alex here who has a request for service," Brian said nervously. You never knew what Anson would do. He didn't answer or show it, but he was interested. He looked the kid over again. He'd heard about Alex for a couple of years but had never seen him. *Didn't look like much, not very big,* Anson thought. It was hard to see how this little kid had earned a reputation as a fighter. It might be fun to find out what he was made of, but a request for service was pretty unusual. He'd find out what the kid wanted, then decide what the price would be. Later he could put him to the test if he was still around.

"Price," Anson said to Alex. His dark eyes glittered dangerously.

Alex told him what he needed and added a blade for the hack saw.

"Why?" Anson said, not really caring but curious.

"My business," Alex said. Anson's lips tightened. He'd killed men for nothing more than not telling him what he asked for, and the kid knew this. *He has balls*, thought Anson, deciding to let it slide.

Anson sat there thinking for a few minutes. A request for service meant he would do any task the Bloods asked him to do, regardless of how dangerous it might be. Many of those who requested service died trying to fulfill the task. This kid would know that.

Anson was having a problem with the Knights up on Thule Street. While they hadn't made any moves at the Bloods, they'd been secretly meeting with the other gangs at night, and that meant they were going to try to take someone's turf. He'd sent several Bloods to get information, but none had returned. He figured he had a mole in his group that was tipping them off. This kid would be perfect. It didn't matter if he didn't return, and if he did, Anson would get the information he wanted at a low price.

"Do you know the Pizza Express on Thule Street?" he asked Alex.

"Yes, that's where the Knights hang out," Alex answered.

"Exactly," said Anson, smiling. "They meet tonight with the other gangs, and I want to know what they are talking about." Alex thought about it for a minute. He knew it was a suicide mission, but he also had a lot of confidence in himself.

"OK," he said, thinking that the reward was worth it. Anson shook his head, sealing the deal. *Kid's not too bright*, he thought. *He should have asked for something worth more than a couple of bucks, but it's OK with me.* He told Alex to wait until dark, then go uptown.

Alex knew Julia would wonder where he was when she got back, but it couldn't be helped. Besides, he didn't have to tell her every time he went out, and he was doing this for her. He thought this only to make himself feel less guilty for making her worry. Alex sat in a dark corner of the Bloods camp, well away from Anson and the other Bloods. He dozed off and on and saw a Blood come in with his parts and the saw blade. Anson looked over at him, and he nodded.

At around six-thirty, Alex decided it was dark enough to try for Thule Street. He didn't know much about the area, so he'd have to be extra cautious. He went out the door and down the block to Center Street. He knew Center Street connected to Thule Street, so he started making his way up. The sun was low now, so he stayed on the darkest side of the street. He'd move a few feet, then stop and watch for anyone around. He'd learned his lesson on Sixth Street when he didn't spot their lookouts and vowed it wouldn't happen again. About four blocks from the start of the

Knights' territory, he met the first Knight. He smelled him before he saw him. The guy was smoking in a doorway on the opposite side of the street, apparently not worried about being seen. Alex moved from dark spot to dark spot, making sure he wasn't seen. He was sure he'd gotten by OK when he saw a movement out of the corner of his eye, this time on his side of the street. It would be harder to get by him unseen this time. He crouched behind a concrete wall, watching the Knight in the corner. The scout was alert, watching both ends of the block. Alex looked around. Across the street were the buildings that connected to the Knights' camp. It was still light enough so he could tell he might be able to get on the roof of the nearest one by climbing up the cracks in the skinny wall section, then climb up behind the old swamp cooler. Maybe he could grab onto the old roof drain to climb the rest of the way up or use the old cooler as a platform. The problem was the noise. He'd have to be very quiet, and he couldn't be seen.

 Alex waited patiently until the scout turned his back and went a few feet back into the storefront, probably to take a leak. He quickly crossed the street and leveraged himself up the wall, using the cracks for purchase. The wall was about eight inches wide, plenty big enough for him to balance on, and he quickly climbed up behind the cooler. He had to be super careful not to be seen or heard. Climbing up on top of the old metal cooler might make noise when he stepped onto it, but it would get him high enough to climb up the rest of the way. Alex went as slowly as he could, easing his weight onto the cooler an inch at a time while making sure the scout couldn't see him. The cooler let out a low groan but not loud enough for anyone to hear. He moved his other leg up and stood up. He was blocked from sight by the porch roof of the building.

 Alex moved slowly and carefully toward the roof drain. The clamps holding it to the wall were rusty, but they looked like they should hold his weight. The terracotta pipe was still intact. He leaned over the edge of the cooler as close to the drain as he could and grabbed for the pipe, his feet still on the cooler. Hanging on, he swung his legs off the cooler and held onto the pipe. It held his weight, and he started pulling himself up to the roof. He had to reach out with one hand to grab the edge of the roof overhang and then let go of the pipe with his other hand. He was at a bad angle, the overhang pushing him away from the pipe. He pulled with his arms and pushed on the clamps with his feet, trying to get his shoulders above the edge of the roof. He got his weight up high enough to pull himself onto the roof and lay there breathing hard.

All the buildings butted up against each other, common walls connecting them. The roofs were all different, though. The one Alex was laying on was rolled rubber, but next door, the roof was tar and gravel. The rubber roof would be quiet, but he'd have to be very careful on the gravel roof. He started going from building to building, being extra careful on the gravel roof. The second building in line was rubber again. That was good because it was quiet, especially since the lookout was straight across the street from that building. Alex thought he might be able to go all the way up the block on the roofs, and if he was lucky, there shouldn't be a lookout near where he'd have to come down. He made it to the end of the row of buildings with no problem, being careful to stay low enough not to be seen from the street. Light was failing quickly, so he needed to hurry. He wouldn't be able to use the roofs in the dark.

At the corner of Center and Spruce, Alex waited, watching the doorways and areas where someone could be hiding. After fifteen minutes, he felt it was clear and started to shimmy off the roof down the drainpipe. This pipe was metal and easier to hang onto than the terracotta pipe before. He made it to the ground and crouched, listening and watching for movement. He saw nothing. He peeked out from behind a parked car. The car looked like it would still run, which meant people were probably nearby.

Thule Street was only two more blocks, but they would be hard ones. He wasn't sure how he would get them up. Being this close to the Knights' hangout, lookouts must be posted close by. He crouched beside the car, trying to figure out a plan. He heard rather than saw the car coming up Spruce Street right toward him. The car he was hiding behind was parked on Center Street, so he would be in plain sight of the approaching car. Not sure where to go, he moved back into a recessed doorway, which barely hid him from sight. The car came up the street and turned left onto Center Street toward Thule. It went about three hundred feet past Alex before its brake lights came up suddenly. Two Knights had stepped out of buildings on the left and stood in front of the car, guns in their hands. Alex used the distraction to move up Center Street until he was almost even with the car and the Knights. He could hear them talking back and forth. The pistols weren't pointed at the car anymore, so they must be part of the gang. Hearing them laughing back and forth, he slipped past the lookouts into another doorway, then the next, then the next.

Chapter 17

Alex made it to Thule Street. On his left, he could see the Pizza Express building. Like Center Street, these buildings used common walls, so Alex thought he might be able to use the roofs again. Getting on top of the first building was easy enough. He had several more roofs to cross to get to the Pizza Express. He started out having trouble seeing some of the debris because the sun was low. Like before, he stayed low so as not to be seen. Alex tripped a few times but managed not to make too much noise or hurt himself. He was one building away from the Knights' building when he heard a soft noise behind him. Alex reacted, not even waiting to figure out what had made the noise. He simply spun around and kicked out, hoping to connect with something. He felt the wind as something whooshed by his head. Alex's foot had connected with someone's midsection at the same time his assailant was swinging a board at Alex's head. The guy was down, gasping for air. For a few seconds, he wouldn't be able to call out, but as soon as he regained his breath, he'd call for help. Alex picked up the two-by-four the Knight had dropped and swung it hard at his head. The lookout went down and didn't move.

Alex listened, but he didn't hear anyone. He decided to keep going. His attacker was still breathing, but he wouldn't be going anywhere for quite a while. Alex made his way to the Pizza Express roof. It was rolled rubber, and Alex searched around for the vent pipes. At each one, he listened to see if he could hear them talking inside. Finally, he found one that he could hear them from and sat down to listen.

Alex was back on Laurel Street. The Bloods had already picked him up, and word went back to Anson that he was coming in. Anson was surprised. The information Alex was bringing was probably worth a hundred times the cost of it, and when word spread that the Bloods had infiltrated the Knights' stronghold, that alone would be worth more than anything Alex had asked for. Anson watched Alex walk toward him.

Not a scratch, he thought. Maybe some of the stories about Alex were true. Alex quickly told Anson what he had heard.

A deal was a deal, and he would honor it, so Anson picked up the bag of parts, the hacksaw blade, and the pipe and handed them to him. Alex took them and turned around to leave, not saying anything. A group of Bloods stood around Alex, waiting to hear what Anson wanted them to do. Alex stood there waiting, ready to fight if he had to. Then he heard, "Take him out, Brian," and the other Bloods melted back.

Alex followed Brian out and down the street.

"I think you got lucky this time, but you'd better not try this again." With that, Brian turned back around and headed up Laurel Street. Alex waited for a few minutes, then started walking down Laurel toward their alley. He turned several times to see if he was being followed, but he saw no one. At the alley, he turned in and went to the back door. He knocked quietly and waited, hoping she was there and that she'd let him in. It took a few minutes until he heard her moving inside. He was nervous standing out there and wanted to get out of the alley.

As soon as the door unlocked, he went through and shut it, locking the door and putting the post in place. Julia had already gone into the kitchen, so he headed there. When he went through the kitchen door, she was standing there waiting for him. She had changed her clothes and was wearing the new top and sweatpants from his mom's clothes. Her hair was down and brushed. She looked beautiful, but she was angry. He could see that she had been crying, but of course, she wouldn't admit it. Any second now, she would lash out at him, so he did what he would normally do in a fight—he struck first.

He walked over to her and put his arms around her. She went rigid, and he was afraid she would try to hit him, but he continued to hold her. After a few seconds, he felt her relax, and her arms go around him, and they stood there embracing. He could feel her body shaking and only then realized she was crying again. He pulled back, and she let him turn her head to face him. He looked into her eyes.

"I won't ever do it again, Julia," he said quietly.

She just looked at him with that hurt look and finally said, "OK."

For dinner, they skipped the last two steaks, deciding to eat them the next day. She had some cheese from the market, and Alex used the old paring knife to cut off the mold and parts that had dried out. They ate the cheese with the leftover oven rolls. After eating, Alex showed her the parts and the pipe. Julia didn't ask where he got them. She was amused at how proud he was of the plumbing stuff, but she didn't know what he was going to do with them and didn't ask. He was back; he was sorry. That's all she needed to know.

It was late now. They hurried to wash up, and both knew they looked forward to the ritual. Julia didn't know why she looked forward to it; maybe it was just having something they did together each night to look forward to. She didn't want to think it might be something else. *Probably both*, she thought. As for Alex, he had no clue. He just knew that he looked forward to this time every night.

When Alex finished, Julia handed him her towel and the shirt to sleep in. He used the towel and hung it up to dry, then donned the shirt. When he finished dressing, he turned toward Julia, and she suddenly hit him on the arm and yelled, "Tag!" then raced out of the bathroom and dove into the bed. Alex was right on her heels. They laughed and wrestled for a few seconds. Alex pinned her shoulders down and sat on her legs, then rolled off and lay next to her, breathing hard. The cat had disappeared, scared by the noise of the running humans.

It hadn't been easy holding her shoulders down; she was very strong. They lay there side by side on top of the blankets. Julia broke the silence first.

"Did you think any more about seeing uptown?" she asked.

This time, he didn't get angry. "How would we do it? We don't have transportation, and it's miles to the downtown area. What if a cop stopped us and wants to know where we're from? What are we gonna tell him?"

"I'm not too worried about that," she replied. "We can blend in. They don't just stop kids unless they think there's a reason."

"How will we blend in? We'd probably stick out like sore thumbs."

"I'll figure that part out, Alex, trust me." He had nothing to say to that.

That night, Alex was restless. Something was bothering him, and he wasn't sure what. Some sixth sense was telling him there was trouble ahead. Around 2:00 a.m., he woke up suddenly, lying quietly while he tried to figure out what had disturbed him. Then he realized it wasn't something he'd heard; it was Julia. She was lying on her left side, her body pressed against him and her right arm across his chest. Her right leg was draped across the top of his legs. He could feel her breath on his neck and her breasts rise and fall against his arm. He thought about moving away but realized he really didn't want to. He lay there in the dark, enjoying her closeness.

Julia opened her eyes in the dark. She wondered what Alex would do when she moved close to him, and she was happy he didn't pull away. She closed her eyes and drifted off to sleep.

Alex woke up around daylight. He still had a nagging feeling that something was wrong but didn't know what. Julia had rolled over on her left side sometime in the night, so he slipped out of bed, trying not to wake her. He padded into the bathroom, peed, washed his face and teeth, and came back out. It was Sunday, and even though the group kids didn't work, Sunday had always been a low-key day. Alex was going to wash his clothes today, maybe clean up the kitchen for Julia and finish hooking up the water to the kitchen sink. He came back into the room and picked up his dirty pants, shirt, and socks. He took them to the bathroom and put them in the corner. He needed to ask Julia how she washed clothes, whether in the toilet or the sink.

When Alex came out of the bathroom, Julia was sitting up. She stretched and yawned, smiled at him, and climbed off the bed. She went past him to the bathroom. Alex turned the light on and looked at the parts he'd gotten. He hoped he'd be able to break the old pipe loose and connect it to the water supply. He rarely ate breakfast, but this morning he was hungry, so he opened the refrigerator to see what they had to eat. Two of the steaks were still in there, and a few rolls were left. He took out the rolls and put them on the old cookie sheet, then lit the oven as Julia had shown him. They didn't have butter, but he didn't care. He popped the rolls into the oven to bake. The heat from the old oven felt good in the chill of the early morning.

Julia came out looking clean and brushed.

"What are you cooking?" she asked him, opening the oven to look for herself. "Rolls, good. I have a small jar of honey that we can put on them."

"I've never had honey," he said.

"It's sweet," she said. "You'll like it."

Alex opened the jar lid with a knife. They spread honey on the rolls and ate them with water to drink. Alex and Julia each had one roll, and they split the third.

"That was delicious," Alex said, wiping his sticky fingers on his shirt.

"No, silly, wash your hands. Don't wipe them on your shirt."

He blushed and got up to do as she said. When he came out, she was sitting on the bed again, leafing through a different book.

"I'd like to wash my clothes today," he said. "Where do you wash them?"

Julia had picked up the soap pieces Alex brought back from the apartment building and put them under the sink in the bathroom. "I usually wash them in the sink with soap, rinse them, and hang them in the bathroom. There's a thin rope I hook up to hang them on. You'll see it hanging on the wall by the old bathtub. If I wash the blankets or have a big load of clothes, I use the old bathtub with buckets of water, but it would have to be cleaned out first."

"I'll just use the sink. I don't have much," he said.

"Do you want me to wash your clothes for you?" Julia asked him.

"No, I can do my own but thanks." *Why would she wash my clothes*, he wondered to himself.

"You need to wash your nightshirt because you got honey all over it," she told him.

"I have nothing to put on," he said.

She just shrugged.

Alex decided to wait until it got warmer to wash the clothes. Even with the heat from the old stove, it was too chilly to sit around naked. He decided to work on the plumbing instead.

"Is there anywhere you have to go today?" he asked her.

"No, I usually hang out here on Sundays," she replied.

"Good," he said, "we'll make it a workday here, OK?"

"OK," she said, secretly pleased.

Alex put his shoes on without socks. He didn't want to walk around in the basement barefoot. Like most of the kids here, his feet were tough from going barefoot in the summer, but too much debris was on the floor, and he didn't want to step on a piece of glass or a nail. He saw Julia snickering at his outfit—a shirt that came to his knees, bare legs, and sneakers. He scowled at her, but she just smiled broader. Alex picked up the piece of pipe and bag of parts and headed down to the basement. The cat was back in his spot, still watching Alex guardedly.

Downstairs we went over to the section of the pipe he wanted to remove. He put the pipe wrench on the union nut and tried to turn it. As expected, it was frozen in place. Alex looked for a piece of pipe to use as a cheater and saw a two-foot section of an inch-and-a-half pipe over by the doorway. *Perfect*, he thought. Alex put the piece of pipe over the handle of the pipe wrench and pulled hard. The nut came loose, and he turned it until the union separated. He unhooked the section of pipe and connected a ninety-degree fitting to the pipe, then threaded his new piece of pipe into it. He removed the union from the old pipe. He put another ninety on the end of the new pipe. He had a six-inch nipple to connect to the water supply with a tee. He'd use the old union there. Now he had to find out how to shut the water supply off so he could connect it.

Alex followed the water supply pipe through the basement of the neighboring building. It went through the wall near the escape path, so he opened the door and went outside. He walked up the path until he saw the junction for the water supply. *Must be here*, he thought. The path walls were about waist high, so he could easily reach the junction box. He pried the lid off using a rusted nail he'd picked up. It came up easily. Inside was a valve with a handle. He pulled the handle up, shutting off the water, then went back to the basement, leaving the junction lid off.

Inside, he found the union connecting the supply line to the inside pipes. Using the cheater, he loosened the union and began to turn the pipe to unscrew it. Alex removed the pipe from the coupler, then unscrewed the coupler and replaced it with the tee fitting. He didn't have any plumber's tape or anything to coat the threads with, so he hoped it wouldn't leak too badly. Alex threaded the new pipe into the tee, reconnected the supply pipe to the other end, and tightened the union. He tightened all the fittings as much as he could.

OK, here goes nothing, he thought, heading back to the junction box. Outside, he turned the supply valve handle slowly, listening to the water start to flow back into the building. He waited, hoping he'd hear the water stop, meaning there were no leaks. Finally, it did. Alex put the cap back on the box and went back inside, locking the basement door behind him. In his basement, water dripped rapidly from one of the unions running to the kitchen sink. He put the wrench on the union nut and pulled. It didn't budge, so he picked up his cheater and put more pressure on it. The nut turned a fraction, and the dripping almost stopped. *Good enough*, he thought, not worrying about the tiny leak.

When Alex got back upstairs, Julia was looking at him happily. "Wow, will it really work?" she asked. He didn't answer but went over to the sink. Nothing came out of the hot water faucet, of course, but when he turned on the cold water, it spat and burped until the air was out of the line. Then a steady stream of water flowed out. He made sure the drain wasn't leaking and turned the water off.

"How's that?" he said, proud of himself.

She got off the bed and put her arms around his neck and kissed him quickly on the lips. "Wonderful," she said and let him go.

They decided to wash their clothes in the new sink. Julia got a rag and a piece of soap and started scrubbing the sink while Alex went into the bathroom and gathered his dirty clothes. He came out, putting the clothes down by her, and said, "Where are your dirty clothes? I'll bring them over." She pointed to the old dresser and said, "In the bottom drawer." He went over, the old cat standing up, ready to run. Alex ignored the cat and got the clothes out of the drawer. He turned away, and the cat settled back down. He brought her clothes over and piled them on top of his. Julia was done cleaning the sink.

"How about if I wash and rinse and you hang them?" she said. He nodded yes and went into the bathroom to string up the clothesline. When he came back out, she was happily filling the left sink with cold water.

"I'll wash in this one and rinse in this one," she said. "The clean clothes will be on this counter if you would hang them for me."

"Sure," he said. She held out her hand to him, but he didn't understand what she wanted. Then he realized she wanted his shirt with the honey on it. He took it off and handed it to her, standing there naked. The chill was pretty much gone, but he got goosebumps anyway.

"I'll wash our nightshirts first," she said, removing her shirt. "Maybe you can figure out a way to hang them by the stove so they dry faster?" Alex walked over to the stove, and like in the bathroom, there were nails on the walls. "I can hang them here. Do you want me to turn on the oven?"

"Yes," she replied. "Turn the oven on low and leave the door open a little." He did as she suggested.

This is kinda fun, Alex thought, picking up the clean clothes to hang as she finished them. He watched her wash and rinse, admiring how she moved and how beautiful her body was.

Oh no, he thought as he felt himself getting excited. He turned and went into the bathroom, splashing cold water on his face. That helped. He'd have to avoid looking at her or thinking about her body to try to control his body. He went back into the kitchen, keeping his eyes on the sink, the walls, the bed, anything but on her. Julia didn't notice until she turned around and he studiously looked away from her.

"Something wrong?" she asked quizzically, not understanding why he was avoiding looking at her.

"No, no, everything's fine. Let me get those clothes, and I'll hang them up." He quickly walked over to the piled clothes, gathered them up, and took them into the bathroom. She watched him go.

Alex stayed in the bathroom, concerned about going back out there. After a few minutes, Julia came into the bathroom looking for him.

"What's wrong, Alex?" she asked, concern on her face.

He tried not to look at her. "Nothing, everything's fine," he replied nervously.

"Alex, look at me," she suddenly demanded.

Reluctantly, he did. She stood there right in front of him, and he couldn't ignore the effect her body had on him. He began to get an erection, but there was nothing he could do. He saw her eyes move down to his penis as it swelled and began to rise up. He watched her as she watched him grow. When he was fully erect, she looked up at him.

"I can't help it," he said in an anguished voice.

She moved toward him. "It's OK, I understand." Her eyes were shining. "I feel the same way about you. You just can't tell," she told him. "I don't know what we're going to do. This is natural, I know, but we have to decide how to deal with it. I don't want to worry about being naked in front of you or you in front of me. I'm attracted to you. I think about you all the time, and I think you feel the same way."

"I do, Julia. I just don't know much about the physical stuff."

"Neither do I, Alex, so we'll just have to learn together. Until then, just be natural around me and don't worry about that." She pointed at his erect penis. "I'm flattered."

Julia went back to the other room. Alex went over to the sink. He splashed cold water on his face again. He heard what she said, but he was still embarrassed. The water worked. When he went back out, she was dressed in the shirt again. He went over and took his down from the nail. It was a little damp, but that was OK; at least he was covered, just in case.

Alex had to laugh. Julia was so happy with the kitchen sink she was almost singing. *Girls are easy to please,* he thought, smiling. Then he remembered their conversation in the bathroom, and the smile disappeared. *What am I going to do?* he wondered.

Alex dressed when his clothes dried and went out into the dining room. He walked around, looking at all of the restaurant equipment piled up. There wasn't much to work with. He wondered what they needed. The kitchen was big, so they had plenty of room. The cookstove would keep them warm, and in the summer, they would leave the basement door open so the cool air from down below would come up—that is if they were still here in summer. He could always find an old fan somewhere.

Now it was October, still warm during the day in El Paso. Nights and mornings got a little chilly, but that was OK. They both needed clothes, but that was something they'd work on together. One thing they didn't have was any money. Down here, everything was done by barter, but if she really wanted to go uptown sometime, he'd need cash. He'd have to figure out how to get some.

Alex found a bunch of wood screws that had fallen out of a cardboard box. He gathered them up, figuring they'd come in handy sometime. He went back into the kitchen and down to the basement. Julia must be in the bathroom because he didn't see her. Downstairs, he went to the old cabinet and started cleaning off the shelves. He was taking it back from the rats, and he'd use this locker to keep his building materials in. The screws went on the shelf. He looked around in the old basement. *Maybe I can build a workbench down here*, he thought. There's plenty of room and scrap wood and even some old dining tables. He'd think about it. He shivered and remembered he wasn't really dressed. Besides, he shouldn't be walking around down here barefoot.

Alex went back upstairs. Julia was in the kitchen, emptying out her backpack. "Are you going somewhere?" he said. "I thought we were going to hang out today."

"I thought I'd go over to see Laura and check the grapevine. They might have a line on food or something. I'll only be gone for a few minutes. Maybe the clothes will be dry by then."

"Do you want me to go with you?" Alex asked.

"No thanks, I won't be long, and I'll get more information if you're not there." He knew she was right, but it still hurt a little.

"I'll make us some lunch while you're gone," he said.

Julia squeezed his hand and picked up the empty backpack. "Lock me out, OK?"

"Sure," he replied and got up to follow her out, still barefoot.

Julia found Laura with some of the group kids by the old donut shop. She knew they liked to hang out there because they could see anyone coming from a long distance. The kids greeted Julia, but she could tell they looked at her differently since she'd hooked up with Alex. Laura and Beth were over by the archway, and Laura was brushing Beth's hair.

"Hey," Julia said, walking over to them.

Laura looked up at her. "Hey," she said back.

"Food?" Julia said, falling back into the single syllable talk the groups used.

"No," Laura said.

"News?" Julia asked her, following group protocol.

"Yes, and bad for you." The fact that Laura almost used a complete sentence meant something was very wrong.

Laura stopped brushing Beth's hair and put the brush down. "Come," she said to Julia and stood up. Julia followed her as Laura went around the building to the back.

"Bad trouble for Alex and for you. Dead Knight, Bloods," said Laura.

Julia felt her stomach rise, and she almost vomited. She felt dizzy. "Not true, Laura, tell groups," Julia said.

Chapter 18

Julia didn't wait for a response. She turned and hurried away from the shop back to their nest, being extra careful that no one was following her. She knocked on the door, hoping Alex wasn't out or downstairs. She heard footsteps from inside and the sound of the post being removed. The door opened, and she quickly stepped inside.

"Lock it quickly, Alex," Julia said and headed back to the kitchen. He heard the strain in her voice, so he hurried, locking up quickly and went after her.

When he came into the kitchen, Julia was facing the dresser with her back to him. He could see her shoulders shaking. Was she hurt? Alex went over to her and put his hand on her shoulder, turning her to face him. Tears were streaming down her face, but she didn't make a sound. He stepped toward her, putting his arms around her and pulling her close. She didn't resist. Holding her tight, he could feel the sobs wracking her body, and finally, she let herself go. They stood that way for several minutes, neither speaking. He could feel her body finally relaxing, and when she finally spoke, the words were muffled by his shoulder, but they still chilled him.

"Alex, the Bloods say you killed a Knight on the roof at Pizza Express. They have a pact with the Knights. If they find you, you know what will happen." She shuddered again.

Alex loosened his grip on her and stepped back. He looked at her and said, "Julia, it's not true. I fought with a Knight on that roof, but he was alive when I left."

She was silent for a minute, then said, "The Bloods set this up. They want more territory and use you as the way to get it somehow."

"I'll go to the Bloods and tell them what happened," Alex said.

"No, they won't believe you, and if the Knights catch you, they'll just give the Bloods a dead Alex. You have to stay away from both of them."

"You need to go, Julia. Go stay with your group until this is over. I can't let them find you with me, and you know they'll find me sooner or later."

She looked straight into his eyes. "No, Alex, I won't leave you, and whatever happens, happens to us both." He could hear the steel in her voice.

"We need to think about this and make a plan." She took his hand to lead him over to the bed. Climbing up, she sat there and motioned him to join her. Julia knew the only hope they had was to leave old El Paso. They would have to find a way to get uptown. She knew they could do it, looking at what they had survived living here. The problem was convincing Alex. He had a deathly fear of uptown and thought he was beneath those living there. How silly, most of them wouldn't last five minutes down here, but how could she convince him that he was worth more than any ten of them? She had to think of a way.

Julia was right. As Alex sat on the bed in silence, his mind went through the options open for them. Just as Julia had figured out that uptown was their only choice, Alex came to the same conclusion. *But how?* he thought. The people there were different. They looked different and talked different, and he and Julia would stand out in a second. They'd have to find a way to blend in. He looked at her sitting there next to him and took her hand.

"Uptown," he said, and she nodded yes.

Chapter 19

Sitting in the makeshift office upstairs, Anson smiled when he thought about Alex. It was so easy to arrange for the blame to fall on him for the death of the Knight. He knew the Knights would want immediate revenge, and the offer from the Bloods to help find the killer was sheer genius. With one simple killing, he had moved the Bloods a big step closer to taking over the Knights' territory, and they would never see it coming.

He looked out of the office window that faced the depths of the old warehouse. About twenty tattooed youths in T-shirts and jeans lounged around on the crates and stacks of pallets. Anson knew that if he got up and went out there, he could have them on the street doing his bidding in seconds. His musing was interrupted when he saw Rusty standing in the open doorway, waiting for permission to enter. Anson knew Rusty would stand there silently all day without coming in unless he gave him the go-ahead. This was Anson's inner sanctum, and no one would enter or disturb him without an invite, not even Luke.

"Speak," Anson said, not turning around to look at Rusty.

"Boss, you know if them Bloods get to the kid first, they'll make him talk, and then they'll know we set the whole thing up. They might not know we killed the Knight, but sooner or later, they'll figure it out."

"That's why we're going to get to him first," Anson said, spinning his chair around to look at his street lieutenant. "I want every man in the warehouse on the street in five minutes looking for the kid. If you find him, kill him on the spot. I don't want him opening his mouth to nobody." He thought for a minute.

"I want you to check with the groups. See what you can find out about where this Alex lives and who he hangs out with." Anson turned back around to look out the window, watching Rusty's reflection leave the door frame. Rusty went down to the warehouse floor and called the Bloods together. Anson couldn't hear what he was saying, but as he expected, the soldiers got their weapons and were out the door in just a few minutes.

That ought to take care of our friend Alex, he thought, dismissing the issue to consider more pressing matters.

Julia stepped into the alley quickly, heading back to the groups to find out what was going on. Alex was upset that she was going, but they needed to know about the search before they tried to start uptown. Alex couldn't go.

"Julia, just see Laura and get the info, then get out of there. We don't know if they're looking for you too."

Julia remembered the look on his face—fear, guilt, and something else, something really important to her. She kissed him quickly on the lips and went out through the kitchen door before she changed her mind. She didn't look to see if he was following her, but she knew he would. They had no other choice.

Julia got to the corner of Laurel and Fourth and quickly ducked behind a rusted car. She heard rather than saw the two guys coming toward her on the street. She moved around the car as they passed, staying hidden. She could smell their cigarettes and caught a few words from their conversation. She heard her name, and that ended her trip down to the groups. One of the kids had told them about her and Alex, so there was no reason to go there. They no longer had friends in this part of El Paso.

Alex was surprised when he heard the quiet tap on the street door. *How could she be back so quickly?* he wondered, peeking into the alley to make sure it was Julia. He lifted the brace and let her in, closing and locking the door quickly behind her. Julia motioned him to follow her, not speaking in case someone was close by outside. They went into the kitchen and sat on the bed.

"They know about me, Alex," she said, taking his hand. "It's nobody's fault. They're all scared of what the gangs might do to them."

"I know, Julia. I just feel bad for getting you into this."

"Don't. Even in this situation, there's no place I'd rather be." He looked at her, saying nothing. With a sigh, he got off the bed.

"We have to pack and go now. Sooner or later, they'll find us somehow if we say any longer. We take only the minimum. We might have to run. He turned and went into the bathroom to put the soap and their meager bath items in his old backpack. Julia went through the drawers, picking two changes of clothes for the both of them. Then she went into the kitchen and looked through their food supplies, grabbing whatever was portable and wouldn't spoil. They wouldn't have time to forage until they were clear of the gangs."

"It's too early to leave yet. We need the dark," she told him. "I'm going to make our last meal here. I don't know when we'll be able to stop again."

"OK," Alex said, still in the bathroom. Julia went to the old stove and lit the front burner. She decided to make their last meal as good as she could and got out the last steak, some old vegetables, and an old package of spaghetti noodles. They didn't have spaghetti sauce, so she put the last of their butter in a pan and fried the noodles, adding garlic, salt, and pepper. The steak got the same treatment, and then she sorted through the vegetables, picking the freshest and leaving the rest in the sink. She threw them in with the meat, cutting up the last garlic clove and throwing it in. It smelled good; hopefully, it would taste OK. At least they could leave on a full stomach.

Alex had changed into his old tennis shoes, double tying the laces so they wouldn't come undone. "Go change. I'll watch the food," he said, taking the fork from her. She did as he asked, picking the loosest clothing and her old running shoes in case they had to make a break for it.

"What about weapons?" she asked him.

"Has to be pretty light, something you can run with. We'll just want to slow them down so we can get away." She thought a minute and rummaged in the old dresser for her club, the one she'd used on the boys. Alex smiled when he saw what she had in her hands, remembering how effective the club had been against the two group boys. His choice was harder. Most of the gang members had guns, not something he had access to. They'd be defenseless against them if they were caught in the open. He decided to take his stick, a four-foot piece of an inch-and-a-half hickory curtain rod. He was deadly with it in close quarters, and if necessary, he could throw it like a spear. After dinner, he'd sharpen one end and harden it over the gas burner. It would have to do.

Chapter 20

Alex looked out their little spy panel for a long time, making sure nobody was in the alley. They had decided that the best way to bypass the gangs was to go along the border until they were well past the blocks controlled by the groups and the gangs. Then they'd angle uptown until they were swallowed by the busier parts of town.

They had checked each other, trying to look and dress as much like the uptowners as they could with their meager clothing choices. They were not really sure how they should look to blend in; they just tried to look as plain and clean-cut as they could. Julia cut Alex's hair, and he scrubbed and shaved. She brushed her hair, leaving her caps behind. He told her he thought they looked presentable. *Actually*, he thought, *she looks real pretty.*

They slipped out into the alley, staying close to the walls as they made their way to the intersection. It was early evening, and shadows from the lowering sun helped screen them from prying eyes. The plan was to get past the gang haunts as quickly as possible. They hoped most of the scouts would be off the street seating because this was the quiet period before uptown folks came looking for a good time.

Alex was in the lead. He would move from cover to cover, motioning Julia to come once he knew they were clear. They'd reached Ninth Street, two blocks past the Blood's stronghold. Still in a dangerous area, he was on high alert, but he didn't see one of Anson's scouts hiding beside a building across the street.

Freddy saw the kid and ducked back behind the wall. The kid was alone, so Freddy figured he could take him down. Anson had said "dead or alive," and dead would be that much simpler. He pulled the automatic from the back of his jeans and checked to see if there was a round in the chamber. The kid was moving south, trying to be quiet and blend in with all the junk so as not to be seen.

Too bad, kid, Freddy thought as he slid back the receiver and chambered a nine-millimeter round. He ran back down North Street, vain to Myrtle Street, then doubled back up Octavia to get in front of Alex. He'd catch him as he crossed North Tays to Magoffin Street, and that would be that. Freddy got to the corner of Octavia Street just as Alex was crossing to Magoffin Street. He leaned against the building, steadying his aim. The shadows would keep him hidden from Alex as long as he was still.

Alex had no idea that he had been seen or that he was walking into an ambush. After he crossed to Magoffin, he stopped, looking in all directions for any sign of trouble. He saw nothing, so he turned back to where Julia was hiding and waved her all clear.

Freddy saw that Alex was looking away from him, so he decided it was time to take him out. He moved slightly to get a better angle at the kid's back. Julia saw the shadow on the wall behind Alex move and instantly knew that somebody had Alex in their sights. Giving up all semblance of stealth, she screamed, "Look out!" and dove behind a rusting refrigerator. Alex moved with lightning speed, but Freddy fired as soon as the kid started to move. The kid went down.

Knowing his shot wasn't perfect, Freddy broke cover to finish the kid off. He kept an eye out for the girl, but he wasn't too worried about her. He'd deal with her next. As he got closer to where Alex went down, he grew cautious. He knew the kid was a fighter, but he was wounded, if not dead, and wouldn't present any real problem.

He could see the kid's feet sticking out where he had fallen facedown. Freddy kept the gun pointed at the kid's body. He could see a lot of blood and a ragged hole in the kid's shirt just above his left hip.

Probably blew a kidney out, Freddy thought as he came up to the kid. But before he could finish him off, Alex swept Freddy's legs out from under him and was on him before he hit the ground. Pinning his gun hand down with his knee, Alex slammed Freddy's head into the pavement several times until the back of Freddy's skull cracked. He fell back just as Julia reached him.

"Are you OK?" she said, seeing the bloody, torn shirt. "Alex, talk to me," she cried, pulling his head into her lap.

"I'll be OK," he said slowly. "Help me stop the blood." She ripped a strip from his undershirt and balled it up.

"Put this against the wound to slow the bleeding." She handed Alex the ball of material.

"I need one for the other side too," he said haltingly, "then something to hold them in place. We've got to hurry. The gunshot will bring attention."

Julia looked around for something to bind him with. Freddy was a big boy, and he wore a thick leather belt. She went over to the body and started to remove the belt. It was hard work; he was heavy, and his bowels had let loose. That smell, combined with the sickening smell of blood, almost made her faint as she wrestled the belt from his limp body.

Alex was pale from loss of blood, but he was still conscious, keeping pressure on the wounds. The exit wound was a ragged hole, much larger than the entry wound, so Freddy must have been using dumdums. Alex kept himself from passing out, knowing Julia would need his help and they would have to flee. Finally, Julia got the belt loose and went back over to Alex. She saw how pale he was and knew he needed a hospital, but that was out of the question. They had no way to call for help, so she would just have to bind the two wads of material and hope it controlled the bleeding. She slipped the leather belt around him, moving the leather directly over the two wounds. She heard Alex take a shuddering breath as she tightened the belt, but he didn't say a word.

When she was finished, she asked him if he could stand.

"I'll need help getting up," he rasped.

"OK, ready?" she asked, getting her arms under his armpits.

"Lift." Alex strained to raise himself up as Julia lifted with all her might. Fortunately, he wasn't too heavy, and together, they managed to get him to his feet. Julia wouldn't let go until he stopped swaying.

"OK, let's move," Alex said, slowly turning to face Octavia Street. "We need to get out of here as fast as we can." Wincing from the pain, he took a couple of stumbling steps and then gained his rhythm. With Julia's help, they headed up the street, no longer trying to hide their presence.

Chapter 21

They had gone five blocks, and Julia couldn't help noticing his breathing was getting more ragged as he put more and more of his weight on her. She spotted an old grocery store with the front door partially hanging open.

"In there, Alex," she said, trying to steer him to the doorway.

"No, we haven't gone far enough yet. They'll find us for sure." He was trying to pull back, but he was too weak to fight her. She kept pulling, almost dragging him to the store and in through the door.

She let Alex slide down to sit on a plastic bucket.

"Stay here while I look around," she said, heading back farther into the store. There were old crates and boxes everywhere, long since emptied out. The rats had made nests of everything they could chew and drag away. The odor of their urine was strong. She held her breath as much as she could as she went deeper into the old store. An old wooden staircase went down into the basement, but Julia had no interest in that area. Tiny feet scurried about as she went deeper into the dark store. A noise above her head made her look up, and she noticed a high landing or loft of some sort, almost invisible in the darkness. An old ladder lay on the floor near the wall, and Julia dragged it over, struggling to raise it up and prop it against the landing. The dust she had disturbed swirled around her nose and mouth, making her cough.

"Are you OK?" she heard Alex say weakly.

"I'm fine. Be quiet," she called back and made sure the ladder was secure. Climbing up rung by rung, she reached the platform, which was stacked with old tarps and broken fruit boxes. She climbed off the ladder, being careful of the landing, but it seemed sturdy. Holding her breath,

Julia pushed and kicked the debris to the far corner, giving her a clear space of about ten feet. Satisfied, she climbed down the ladder and went back to Alex.

"I found us a hiding spot," she told him. She couldn't help but notice how pale he was. He smiled weakly and tried to stand up but needed her help to get to his feet. Alex knew he couldn't go much farther, and as much as he hated closed spaces, he really had no choice but to find a place to hide.

With Julia's help, he went back into the store until they reached the ladder.

"Up there," she said, pointing to the overhead platform. She went up first so she could help him onto the landing. Alex took a deep breath and started climbing up the rungs. Halfway up, he stopped, nauseous from the effort. Willing himself on, he reached the landing. Julia reached out, and between the two of them, Alex made it a few feet in and collapsed. Julia put her jacket under his head.

"Just stay put. I'm going back down to get some supplies and erase our tracks."

Seeing that he was as comfortable as he was going to get, she climbed down the ladder. She figured they had a couple of hours until Freddy was missed and the Bloods came looking. They were only a few blocks from where she'd start running into people, although they weren't the kind of people she'd want as neighbors. Most of them were squatters, trying to live off the grid but closer to some of the amenities that uptown could offer. Julia went up Octavia, then crossed to Pelem Avenue, staying in the deepening shadows.

There, she thought when she saw a mother and several young girls sitting on the steps of an old tenant building. Cautiously she approached them, not wanting to startle them. She got within ten feet of them and stopped.

"Excuse me," she said, making all three jump. "Just looking for some water." She had two dollars that she had saved over several years, and she had hoped to buy food with it, but Alex needed the help now.

"Who you, child?" the mother said, her arms wrapped around the children protectively.

"Just somebody that needs some help. I mean no harm." Julia stepped out of the shadows so they could see her better.

"It's just a girl," the oldest of the children said. The mother relaxed a little.

"I ain't got no charity, missy. Don't have no extra, nothing."

"I just need some water and maybe some food. I can pay." When Julia said "pay," the woman suddenly looked interested.

"Ya know, water ain't free either. Maybe I could get you some if you got money. Don't have much food. Maybe some dry bread's all."

"That's fine. How much?"

"Five dollars for the bread and water. Gotta pay for the container too, understand?"

"I only have two dollars," Julia said, showing her the two bills.

The woman was quiet for a minute. "Well, guess that'll have to do then. You got what you got." She stood up and told the kids to stay on the steps as she went inside the old tenant house. Curious, they stared at Julia, taking in her clothes and shoes.

"You live on the street?" the oldest child asked her, curiosity getting the best of her fear.

"Just for now," Julia said, smiling at the girl.

"We're gonna move uptown and live in a big house," the youngest suddenly blurted out. "Momma told me." Julia and the oldest girl exchanged looks.

"I bet you will, and you'll have new clothes and lots of toys too," Julia said. The young girl smiled broadly, showing her missing teeth, while the oldest smiled her appreciation for the lie. The door opened, and their mom came out holding a quart jar of water and half a loaf of dried bread.

"Best I can do for two dollars, missy," she said, putting her left hand out to Julia for the cash. Julia gave her the two-dollar bills and took the bread and water. All three turned to go back inside.

"I liked her, Momma," the oldest girl said as they melted back into the shadows.

Julia backtracked to the store, being careful to watch for anyone that might be looking for them. She ducked inside and quickly climbed the ladder to where Alex was lying. He hadn't moved at all. She wanted to wash his wounds with the water but didn't have any clean rags. She quickly took off her blouse, then her undershirt and put her blouse back on. She ripped her undershirt into pieces of rag. Getting out the little piece of soap she had brought, Julia poured a little of the water onto the rag, then rubbed the soap on it. She unbuttoned Alex's shirt. He never woke up as she tried to take it off.

The blood had dried, and the wad of material was stuck to the wound in front. She thought for a minute, then took the jar of water and poured some directly onto the undershirt material covering the wound, working the material back and forth as gently as she could. Finally, it came loose, and when she removed it, blood started flowing from the wound again. Julia used the wet rag and soap to clean it as best she could. She knew if she put a piece of shirt on it for a bandage, it would just stick to the wound again. She closed his shirt, making a tent over the wound. The blood flow had slowed to a trickle. She didn't know how to turn him over to get to the exit wound, so she let him be.

Julia climbed back down the ladder and went to the front of the store. She found an old broom with a broken shaft and began erasing their footprints from the dust. When she had backed all the way to the ladder, she started climbing up. At the landing, she stepped off the ladder and stopped.

How am I going to get the ladder up here? she wondered. Looking over at Alex lying helpless and fighting for his life, she knew she would do it somehow. Fifteen minutes later, an exhausted Julia lay down beside Alex, her head resting on the backpack.

Chapter 22

Rusty listened to Butch talk about their search for the two kids. Butch said Freddy hadn't checked in yet, but that didn't bother Rusty. Freddy was unreliable when he was using, which was most of the time. If it wasn't for Freddy's brother Raul, Anson would have gotten rid of Freddy a long time ago. But Raul lived uptown and ran distribution for Anson. Besides, Raul was a stone-cold killer, and Anson preferred to have that kind of talent on his side.

Rusty was positive that the two kids had made a break across the border to Mexico. That made sense, Anson thought. He stopped Butch in the middle of his report.

"Butch, I want you and Casey to cross over. Find Miguel and tell him we're putting a bounty on the kids. We think they crossed. Tell him to spread the word." Butch got up and went out the door.

"Frank, Jack, you two go back up to where Freddy was on watch. Find his dumb ass and bring him back here."

Julia wasn't sure how long she had slept. Alex was still, but he was breathing. Something had woken her up. Silently, she lay there in the dark, listening intently. There was a faint glow over by the front door. Then she could hear quiet voices.

"Somebody else got to Freddy, Jack. Ain't no kid gonna take him out, even if he was high. Besides, Rusty says the kids went over the line."

"Yeah, but we're here, so let's look around. We don't, and sure as hell, Anson will have our balls."

"I just hate these dark buildings. You know they're full of rats and who-knows-what. Hey, Jack, shine the light over here. Mine ain't as bright."

Jack shined his light in front of Frank looking for footprints in the dust. "There's the basement. Wanna go down?"

"Naw, nobody's been here for months. Let's go to the next building till we get to the corner, then call it a night." The men turned back toward the door, not realizing their prey was just above their heads.

After searching the other buildings close to where they found Freddy, Jack and Frank went back to the stronghold to report to Anson. Anson agreed that the kids couldn't have taken Freddy out. He called Raul on his cellphone to give him the news about his brother. Raul pumped Anson for information about Alex and Julia even though Anson said they figured the kids went over the border. Anson was just glad he wasn't the one on Raul's shitlist.

Alex and Julia stayed in the dark and the dust until a pale sunrise started to lighten the old store. When it was bright enough for Julia to examine Alex, she gently moved the front of his shirt and, using more of their precious water and soap, washed the area around the wound. The bullet's entry area was bloody and raw but didn't seem to be festering. She placed two rag bundles on each side of the damaged tissue to hold the shirt away from the wound, then buttoned it up to keep the dust out. She leaned back to stretch and saw that Alex was looking at her.

"Hi, Nurse," he said, smiling weakly. He reached out slowly and took her hand in his. "So, what's for breakfast?"

Julia couldn't believe that he was hungry, but it was a great sign. He still had a long way to go, but hopefully, they'd have a little time to rest and regain some strength. She softened the dried bread in some water and gave him chunks a little at a time. There was only enough for one meal, but that would do for now. She could scavenge while he slept.

When Alex had eaten his fill, Julia ate what was left. Alex had fallen back to sleep, so she quietly crawled over to the ladder and lowered it down to the floor. Carefully, she stepped onto the rungs, testing it with her weight to make sure the ladder wouldn't kick out. After reaching the floor, she pulled the ladder down and dragged it back over to the side of the building, hoping that if someone came, they wouldn't notice it.

It was still early, and the rising sun hadn't begun to bake the streets yet. Julia saw a cat slipping inside a door on the deserted building right across from them. It made her think of the cat they had left behind at the restaurant. Plenty of four-legged meals were running around in the old basement, and she had left the water dripping into the kitchen sink. The cat had been living in the old restaurant before she got there, so he'd be fine. She turned right and headed farther uptown, hoping to find food and water. She knew the lady with the kids was tapped out, so she went past the old tenant building and on up to the corner. She was starting to see a few cars traveling the streets, so she had to be extra cautious not to be seen. You never knew who was in them.

Crossing the street, she stopped and quickly ducked behind a wall when she heard voices. They were still some distance away, and she couldn't catch their words. Julia peeked around the wall and saw that there was a rundown corner market just half a block ahead. Two men stood outside the entrance smoking. An alley ran behind the buildings on that block, so she quietly moved from hiding place to hiding place until she was at the entrance to the alley. It was an old blacktop access road with large potholes, but she saw a pick-up truck parked behind the market, so she knew it was being used. There was a trash bin next to the building. She decided to check out the trash bin to see if there was anything edible inside.

Julia stood as close as she could to the walls, making her way as quickly as she could to the trash bin. If anyone turned into the alley or the people smoking in front came outback, she'd be seen. Her luck held, and she made it to the back of the truck. She kneeled behind the tailgate and, seeing no one around, started sneaking toward the trash bin.

Inside was a mound of trash and foodstuffs rotting in the heat. She knew there wouldn't be any trash pickup in this part of town, so the garbage just accumulated until it started spilling onto the alley. The rats loved it. It took just one quick look and smell to know there wouldn't be anything usable in the pile. Julia heard the back screen door of the store open, and she quickly ducked down behind the bin. She listened to the footsteps, ready to run if anyone came in her direction, but they seemed to be going away from her toward the old truck. She heard a crash as something was thrown into the truck bed, then the footsteps headed back to the store, and the door opened and closed. Julia waited for a minute, then cautiously made her way back to the truck. In the back of the truck was a wooden fruit box with some old melons and an onion. There were also several soda bottles with a little soda left in them. Julia grabbed the onion and two of the least-rotten melons, then three of the fullest soda bottles and quickly made her way back to the entrance of the alley. She looked around the corner, and seeing no one outside the store or on the street, she started making her way back to their hideaway.

Alex was still sleeping when she got back. She felt his forehead, but he didn't seem to have a fever. That surprised her. She carefully moved the shirt from the wound on his side, and it seemed to be healing. It was an angry wound, but she could tell that the area around the puncture was starting to scab. Julia used a little more of her water and soap and washed it again, then covered it with the shirt. With nothing else to do at the moment, she lay down next to Alex and slept.

Chapter 23

Alex woke up stiff and sore but relatively OK. He saw Julia sleeping about a foot away and, looking over her to the front of the building, figured it must be early afternoon from the sunshine coming in. Although he didn't want to move, he had to pee, so he had no real choice. Gathering his strength, he levered himself up to a sitting position. The wound screamed at him, but he blocked the pain and stayed in the sitting position. Julia hadn't moved. He struggled to get to his knees, the exit wound tearing open as the rags that were stuck to it pulled the healing skin apart. Alex almost fainted from the pain, but he took a deep breath and stayed still for a few minutes. Then he began shuffling on his knees to the edge of the platform closest to the back wall. After looking around, he urinated off the platform into the shadows, then shuffled back to Julia.

"Stay here a minute so I can clean the wound in the back," she said as she gathered the last piece of clean rag and the last of the water. "I'll help you take off your shirt. Just hold still." Julia unbuttoned his shirt and began slipping it over his left shoulder, then the right shoulder. It was stuck to the exit wound in the back. The material was stiff with dried blood.

"I have to pull the shirt away from the wound, but I'm not sure how to do it," she said. Julia didn't have enough water to soften the shirt. If she just pulled it, she would open the wound, and it would start bleeding. Also, the pain would be intense, and she didn't know how well Alex could handle that.

As if reading her mind, Alex said, "We need some way to soften the dried blood, and we don't have enough water. What about urine? Isn't that supposed to be sterile?"

Julia looked at him blankly, then said, "You want me to pee on your wound?"

Alex stuttered, "Well, uh no, I thought I could pee in a can, and you could pour it on me."

"That sounds disgusting, and I can't believe it will be sterile."

"I know, Julia, but it's all I can come up with. Use the clean rag and what's left of the water to clean it after you pull the shirt off."

Alex looked around the platform for a container. He found an old beer can, but it was full of dust like everything else in the building. Alex didn't know about the half-empty juice bottles Julia had brought back, and she had forgotten about them.

"OK, option B. You'll have to do the honors, Julia."

"Oh, this is stupid." She sighed. "If I do this, you can never tell anyone about it. Promise me."

"I promise." He turned his back to her so she couldn't see him smiling.

"Alex, come over here and sit down. You hold the rag and water. It's really going to hurt when I start pulling the shirt away from the wound."

"I know, so let's just get it over with." He gritted his teeth as she walked behind him, preparing himself. He heard her unbuttoning her pants and, a few seconds later, felt the hot urine as it cascaded down his back.

"OK, that's enough. Don't drown me," he said, half kidding. Julia pulled her pants back up and knelt on her knees, gripping the shirt. She started working it back and forth, the crusted shirt slowly softening from the liquid. Being as gentle as she could, she pulled the material away from around the damaged area, getting closer and closer to the hole in his back. Finally, about two inches of material remained stuck to the wound itself.

Julia knew she was hurting him; she could feel him tense as she pulled, but he didn't make a sound. She had her left hand on his neck to brace herself, and she could feel the sweat on his skin.

"This last part doesn't want to come loose. It's wet, but the scab has healed over the material. I don't know how to get it loose without tearing the scab, and that will make it bleed too much."

"Just leave it. Cut the rest of the shirt off," Alex said weakly. "Take the knife out of my right pocket. I can't lift my arm high enough right now." He leaned over so she could get the knife out of his jeans.

The knife was sharp, and she quickly trimmed the shirt away, leaving only the material that was scabbed over. She could see the wound now. It was an angry-looking jagged hole about three times bigger than the entry wound. It didn't smell infected. Quickly, she used the last of the water and clean rag to wipe the area clean of urine. When she was done, she said, "That's the best I can do. You have another shirt with you. Is it in your backpack?"

Alex was gray; the cleaning had taken what little strength he had saved up. He nodded toward the backpack, and Julia got the T-shirt out and, very slowly and carefully, dressed him. There was very little seepage from the wound, so it would be OK unless he did something strenuous. Right now, he just needed rest and soon some food. She placed the pack so he could use it as a pillow, and she helped him lie down. He was almost unconscious.

For the next two days, Alex rested up on the platform. Julia brought him food, cleaned his wounds, and fought to keep him still. On the third day, Alex was strong enough to shuffle around the platform on his knees. Eager to start moving uptown, he had Julia go down the ladder and scout the street to make sure no one was lurking around. Satisfied, Alex shuffled over to the ladder and sat down, swinging his legs over the edge of the platform. Julia was at the bottom, holding the ladder still in case it tried to kick out. Taking a deep breath, Alex grabbed the closest rail with his right hand and carefully swung his right leg to the rung two feet below the platform. Stretching his body hurt, but he could manage the pain, and he didn't feel any tearing of the wounds.

Slowly he swung his body off the platform onto the ladder, getting his left hand and foot on the ladder rung. He stayed there for a few seconds, getting his breath back. The ladder stayed in place, thanks to Julia. He slowly descended, rung by rung. There was a band of perspiration on his forehead as he finally touched solid ground. Julia quickly put his right arm over her shoulder to help hold him up.

Alex gained strength quickly. They practiced walking to the front door and back a few times, with Julia supporting his weight. Then Alex tried it by himself, gaining speed and balance as he walked back and forth. After about fifteen minutes, Alex told her that they needed to prepare to leave. She left him leaning against the front wall and climbed the ladder back up to their loft to gather what items they would take. There wasn't much.

Chapter 24

It was getting toward evening, the late afternoon shadows just starting to hide the nooks and crevices that Alex and Julia used for cover. Light enough to navigate the semi-empty streets easily, they made their way up South Mesa Street, occasionally passing people walking or sitting on their steps. There were still a lot of empty buildings down here, and the people they encountered were more focused on their own problems than on a couple of ragged kids. That is all except Peter, who watched them with interest from his alley.

Peter was like hundreds of the homeless people who lived in and around lower El Paso—well, almost like them. In his case, his personal relationship with God gave him more purpose than most. Peter's life was all about the Word of God and bringing it to as many souls as would listen. The fact that he relied on drugs to keep his message flowing was beside the point. In fact, he was positive that the drugs were what let him talk to God one-on-one. Hour after hour, he'd sit in front of the West Ruidoso Downs Bus Station and preach the coming of the end and then ask for donations. It never occurred to him that the two didn't exactly go together.

Peter had lived in this same spot for several years, and most of the commuters were used to the wild-looking preacher with the long hair and crazy blue eyes that seemed to radiate some kind of internal secret. Parker, a local street musician, had even written a song about him, calling him John the Baptist.

Peter liked being a local personality, and as a testament to his popularity, he'd been invited to speak at today's rally on Myrtle Avenue. He didn't know what the rally was for, and he didn't really care.

The car hadn't run for years and was now his residence. Known as John the Baptist locally, Peter liked to give sermons on the street whenever he could get more than one person to listen. He was harmless and was tolerated because he was just getting by like most of them. The police ignored him, and he pretty much stayed to himself until the need to preach hit him.

He watched the two strange kids moving up South Mesa. What struck him as odd was the way they moved from shadow to shadow, as if trying to stay out of sight. Peter knew all about being invisible, which is why he was still in relatively good condition. He had nothing anyone wanted and stayed out of everyone's business unless the Word of God was on him. But Peter sensed that there was something different about these two. Not how they looked; everyone down here was well worn and used up. There was just something different about them, especially the boy. He couldn't figure it out. He could tell the kid had been hurt by the way he held himself, but he still moved with quick, fluid movements that somehow radiated animal strength. *Very different from most of the folks around here*, Peter thought. The girl moved the same way but didn't have that air of suppressed violence the boy did. *Interesting*, he thought to himself as he rummaged in the back of the Volvo for his signboards, quickly forgetting about the kids.

"I know I put them here," he told himself. "Ahhh." He pulled two battered cardboard signboards with cloth straps for his shoulders from behind the back seat. Peter pulled the signboards out of the car and leaned them against the front fender of the Volvo, then opened the front passenger door and got inside. It was the wrong time of day for the upper city scum to come hunting drugs, and he should have a little private time left, at least enough to help him get ready for the event.

Peter sat there for a few minutes, looking out of the car windows to make sure no one was watching him. Satisfied, he pulled the folded newspaper from the driver's seat and spread it open on his lap. Then he reached back under the front seat cushion and untaped the makings, being careful to hold them beneath the windows. He opened the leather pouch and spread the contents on the newspaper. He stared at the makings and thought enough for one more ride to glory.

A few blocks away, Lisa stumbled out of the old apartment building; she was still a little high from last night's party. Her left foot wasn't working very well, and she had to focus on putting one foot in front of the other. A soft giggle sneaked out, followed by a sly smile. It had been a good night. She got high and made a little money on that fat guy from uptown, and nobody got hurt. Nowadays, when uptowners came down to party, you should be a lot more careful. Her friends had checked the fat guy out and said he was OK before she met him. Carefully, Lisa made her way toward the alley off Canal Street, where Peter lived in his car.

Peter's eyes were slowly coming back into focus. He was out of dope, but he'd take care of that later. Right now, he was riding the drug wave, and he needed to get his shit together for the rally. God was looking forward to this rally; he had just told Peter this and that Peter needed to do a good job. After putting everything back, Peter opened the door and got out, hanging onto the roof of the car to hold himself upright. He smiled as the wave helped him get his things ready. The two signboards floated over his head and onto his shoulders. He got his donation box from the back seat, and he was set to go. It was five-forty in the afternoon.

Lisa saw Peter standing by his car, the signboards on him and his tip box in his hands. He was just standing there, with the vacant look in his glowing blue eyes that she immediately recognized.

"Train's leavin', train's leavin', all aboard," Peter called to her when he recognized her.

"Looks like the train already left, Peter," Lisa called back and crossed over to his car. They both laughed, sharing the secret. They started to walk toward Myrtle Avenue, where the rally was to be held.

Chapter 25

Alex and Julia had traveled about six blocks. They hadn't run into any problems, and they were well past the Bloods' territory. Still, they were being cautious. The shadows had descended, and soon, the houses and cars would have their lights on. There were no streetlights down this low in town, so it would be even easier for them to find shelter.

"Julia, we need to keep going a while longer, then find someplace we can crash and find food." She turned and looked at him. She could tell he was hurting, and his skin was almost gray. He was pushing it, she knew.

"How about we find someplace around here? The farther uptown we go, the fewer empty buildings there will be," Julia said.

"Good idea. See that old shop across the street? Let's check it out while it's still light enough."

They watched the street from their shadowed corner and, seeing no one about, crossed the open stretch of the road quickly and ducked behind an old car rusting on the curb. After watching the street for a while, they turned and quickly walked up to the old store, cautiously ducking inside. Alex stayed by the door to the street while Julia explored the old shop. Satisfied, she came back to the entryway and motioned him inside.

Peter and Lisa watched the kids disappear into the old butcher shop. Probably bedding down for the night, Peter thought. He told Lisa to wait, and he crossed the street, making his way to within a few buildings from the store. Peter was being careful; it wouldn't do to be surprised by them in some dark corner. But his curiosity and the drugs were pushing him on, and he snuck up to the broken windows where he could see inside.

Julia was making their bed in the cleanest spot she could find. Their backpacks would do for pillows, and she was piling old cardboard on the wood floor as a bed. They would just use their body heat to stay warm, but this time of year, El Paso stayed pretty warm all night.

Suddenly she heard a cry and quickly turned around, thinking Alex had fallen. But Alex wasn't there; he was outside holding his pocketknife to the neck of an obviously terrified man wearing cardboard signs. The man wasn't struggling; he was just standing still as if he had no fight in him.

"Alex, don't hurt him," Julia called. Alex loosened his hold so the man could move.

"Get inside the store. You know what will happen if you try to get away." Julia could see the glow from Alex's eyes, the dangerous light of pent-up violence. The man didn't answer but slowly turned toward the entrance of the store and started to make his way inside, Alex's left hand on his shoulder and the knife against his kidney.

"Sit over there," Alex said, and the man complied.

Alex and Julia looked at him curiously. The man was wild-looking, with hair sticking in every direction like he had put his finger in a light socket. His clothes were old, and the ratty tennis shoes had holes. He was probably in his mid-twenties, but a hard life had added at least ten years. The cardboard signs had verses from the Bible written on them, and crude bolts of lightning had been painted on the top of the signs.

"Why are you following us?" Alex asked him.

Peter looked at Alex, then turned his head to look at Julia. He suddenly smiled, showing surprisingly good teeth for a homeless person.

"Welcome to the neighborhood, friends," Peter cried out, holding his arms up in the air and tilting his head back as if they had just come from heaven.

Great, Alex thought, *another nut case.*

Then Peter started talking about the neighborhood, the people living there, Lisa, his limousine, and God. He rattled on until Alex started to wonder if he should have used the knife on him. Julia seemed fascinated. The guy was obviously harmless, but he could become a liability with his insatiable need to talk. The less attention they drew, the better for them.

Alex interrupted Peter and asked him if he knew where there was any food.

"God will provide," Peter said joyously. "I have to deliver a sermon in a little while, but if you wait, I'll come back and show you where a feast awaits. Better yet, come with me, and I'll share God's bounty with you." The fanatic light was back in his eyes.

Alex and Julia looked at each other. Neither of them believed Peter. "Just wait for my return, friends, and we will eat our fill."

Alex put his knife away, telling Peter he should leave and not to tell anyone about them. Peter stood up and turned to go out the door and back to where Lisa waited. Suddenly turning, he grabbed Alex by the arm and started trying to pull him out into the street. Alex yelled in pain and pried Peter's hand from his arm. Julia quickly stepped between the two men, knowing Alex was about to hurt the unknowing Peter.

"Peter, Alex is hurt. You can't grab him like that."

"Sorry, sorry, I . . . I didn't know, Alex," Peter stammered. "I didn't mean to hurt no one." Even Alex could see the bewildered hurt in Peter's eyes.

"I was just going to show you where the food is if you can't wait till I get back."

"Just show us where the food is when you get back," Alex said in a nonthreatening manner. "And, Peter, we don't want to be seen by a bunch of people, so take us the back way."

Suddenly Peter's bewildered look turned to a conspirator's joy, and with a sly look in both directions, he crossed the street and walked back to where Lisa waited.

"What happened, Peter?" Lisa asked as Peter walked up. "I saw that kid grab you and pull you inside the old store."

"Nothing, Lisa, they were just concerned about who I was. It's all good, and I think I've found two new converts. Gonna go back after the sermon."

Chapter 26

Four blocks away, Gary and Lois were getting ready for the rally.

"I can't believe you invited that crackpot Peter to speak today," Gary told Lois, stacking more pamphlets on the folding table where they could get to them quickly. Lois ignored Gary's comments, being used to his negative attitude about the street preacher.

"Think of it this way, Gary—Peter has his own following, and they'll be here too, so that's just more folks for us to sell. There's even a song about him now."

"Not sure I want to sell anything to somebody who listens to that crackpot," Gary mumbled, setting the folding chairs up behind the table. He straightened up and looked over their setup.

"Lois, help me drag the podium over there by the corner. Rick says he only has enough cable to reach that far." She put her books down and came over to help.

Parker was leaning against the wall, waiting for his time to go on stage. His guitar was in his hands as always, almost an extension of his body. He saw Lisa and Peter walking toward him, and they looked none too stable. A few people in the crowd were businesspeople, but most were just curious onlookers. He recognized a couple of the bus commuters who liked to watch Peter preach. Gary also saw Lisa and Peter walking up, so he turned on the PA and let it warm up. He motioned for Peter and Parker to come up on the platform so he could explain how to use the sound system. He watched Peter carefully navigating the steps up to the platform, and he could tell he was high.

"Christ," Gary mumbled to himself, but there was nothing to do but let him go on. Gary explained how to turn the microphones on and off and how close to hold them. "Peter, you've got exactly fifteen minutes, no more."

Peter just beamed at him like he'd been handed a million bucks.

"I mean it," Gary warned. "We've got a lot of information to cover this evening, and I need you to be done by six-thirty."

Peter nodded his assent.

"Parker, you warm the crowd up with a couple of songs."

Parker moved to the second mic stand and checked the tuning of his guitar. Satisfied, he turned the mic on and did a soundcheck. Clearing his throat, he began playing the *John the Baptist* song:

> *John the Baptist lives in a limousine,*
> *John the Baptist lives in a limousine.*
> *Well, don't you, John?*
> *Don't you, John?*
>
> *Lisa, 33, shares his back seat,*
> *She keeps the place looking clean and neat,*
> *The white lines never lie,*
> *The white lines lie.*
>
> *Lisa is John's only hope,*
> *While John shoots up images of the Pope.*
> *Well, don't you, John?*
> *Don't you, John?*

Peter closed his eyes and silently hummed along. He was pleased that Parker had written a song about him and that some of the crowd was singing along. *God will be pleased*, he thought to himself, not concerned about how the words painted him. Finally, Parker strummed the last stanza of the song, and when he finished, he waited for a few people to stop clapping and began his second tune. At the end of his second song, he turned and nodded to Peter.

Peter moved up close to the first microphone stand and turned the mic on. It was five after six in the evening.

"Brothers and sisters, I welcome you," Peter said, looking at the people and trying to make eye contact with each of them. "God is pleased that we are together on this fine evening. I know because he told me. He said today would be an eventful day, one that we will never forget."

The crowd chuckled at his words.

"Heaven is close and awaits us. Our judgment day is near. All God asks of us is that we believe in him and show our faith by forsaking our earthly shackles." Normally, Peter would hand around the donation box at this point, but today, Peter turned slowly, surveying the crowd, his blue eyes shining with a drug-induced inner light while his hair stood straight up.

"Show our Lord that you believe!" he cried, raising his arms up. "Show him. He awaits your faith!" he screamed, the drug wave taking possession of him again. "Show him. Show him now, and he will reward you with eternal life," he ranted, his body jerking beyond his control. "Lord, I believe, I believe!" he screamed, staring up into the dark sky at the God only he could see. Gary stepped onto the platform and grabbed the microphone from Peter, who was oblivious to his presence.

"Thank you, Peter," Gary said loudly into the microphone, giving Peter a shove toward the stairs. Peter staggered toward them, still not comprehending the world around him.

"Now, folks, I know you're here to learn how we can help save the old theater on Mason Street." He turned and motioned Lois to join him at the podium. "Folks, many of you know Lois and her untiring efforts to save one of El Paso's finest historical . . ."

In a daze, Peter made it back to where Lisa was standing, and they made their way back toward the Volvo. Peter suddenly stopped.

"Lisa, you go on back to the limo. I need to go see those two kids."

"Don't ya want me to come with you?" Lisa asked, a little afraid to leave him alone.

"No, they're really shy. You might scare them off. I won't stay long." Peter turned from Lisa and started walking away toward the old grocery store. Her feelings hurt, Lisa sniffed and watched him shuffle off, then shrugged and turned toward their alley.

Julia saw Peter coming before Alex did. Alex was resting on their homemade bed before they went out looking for food. As Peter got closer, he stopped and motioned for Julia to get Alex and follow him. Sighing, Julia went back inside the store to tell Alex. Alex wasn't very excited about following the street preacher, but Julia thought it might be a good idea. Julia went first, following Peter. Alex lagged behind them a little, continuing to scan the streets. Peter took them through a series of alleys and deserted buildings for a few blocks until he reached the dumpster in the back alley of a rundown Mexican food restaurant. Peter was excited again.

"Can you believe it? They throw this food away!" he exclaimed, lifting up the dumpster lid and showing them scraps from the Mexican lunch plates.

Julia tried to ignore the cigarette butt stuck in the refried beans, but Peter just pulled it out and threw it away, then began eating off the plate with gusto. Alex and Julia had no trouble finding enough unspoiled food to satisfy their hunger too. Alex stuffed a package of two-day-old tortillas in his shirt after checking them for mold. He couldn't afford to get sick in his condition. He marveled at how much food was in the dumpster this far down in Old Town, surprised that there was enough business down here to generate it.

"Most of this food came from their food trucks," Peter said, reading Alex's mind. "They go uptown every morning, and they came back just a little while ago. The trick is to know their schedule 'cause the food doesn't stay here long. Too many hungry people and animals around."

Having eaten their fill, Alex and Julia gathered as much food as they could carry that wouldn't spoil right away.

"We're going back to the store to sleep, Peter. Julia and I are leaving early in the morning," Alex said. "Thank you for your help, but it's time for us to go."

Visibly disappointed at not being invited back to the store, Peter gave them a sad smile and waved as the two young people went on their way.

"God be with you, my friends," he said softly under his breath and turned to go back toward Lisa and the old Volvo.

Chapter 27

Back at the old butcher shop, Julia started packing the food they had brought back. Alex sat down on the cardboard bed and watched her do her work. He was tired, and the wounds were sore but nothing he couldn't handle. He was lucky they weren't infected, probably because of Julia's care.

At ease for a while, Alex began pondering their next move. Up to this point, he had just been reacting, trying to put distance between them and the danger. Now, in this relatively safe place, they had decisions to make. What would he do once they got to where they would try to start a new life? How would they know when they reached the right spot? How would they live, make money, or blend in? He and Julia had a lot to talk about, and they had to do that soon. They couldn't just keep wandering.

While Julia put up the food in newspapers, she was thinking along the same lines as Alex. She knew that he was out of his element and was probably worried about what was coming next. Julia was confident that they would be OK; she just needed to get Alex to think the same way. She glanced over at him sitting on the bed, eyes half-closed. Tonight, she thought, seeing that he seemed more relaxed than he had been since they left the nest.

The light had finally given out. Alex figured it was about eight-thirty, and as he expected, it was still very warm. Julia would use her one change of clothes for covers; he still had the pants he could drape over him. They'd be fine.

Julia was near the doorway, using some water they'd put in an empty juice bottle to wash herself. *I need to do the same*, Alex thought as he watched her try to wash her hair. Fortunately, her hair was short now, so she could let it air-dry. Julia had stripped down to her underpants, and the rising moon let in just enough light for Alex to see her outline. It had been a long time since he'd felt anything but fear and anger, but now that he was relaxed and felt safe, his body was reacting to her almost naked form.

As if reading his mind, Julia called to him to come and wash up. She was right; he certainly needed a good sponge bath, and the wounds needed to be cleaned. This might be their last chance for a while. Alex got up slowly, his body still sore and stiff from sitting, and went over to Julia. She turned toward him and walked up close, unbuttoning his shirt. She reached down and unbuttoned the waist button, then unzipped his pants. She couldn't miss the fact that he was aroused, but she pretended not to notice. Her touch was like an electric shock to Alex, but he held himself back, knowing this was not the right time or place.

With her help, he managed to get his pants down to his ankles. He wasn't wearing underwear. It was easier to use his feet to pry off his shoes rather than trying to bend down to do it. His socks were a bigger problem, but Julia solved that by kneeling down and sliding them off, one at a time. She stood up, holding the socks away from her face.

"These are getting washed or burned," she stated, not asking permission. She dropped them near where her clothes were dropped.

"If we can get more water, we could wash all the clothes. We don't know when we'll get another chance, and we're going to be around people, so we need to clean up our act."

Alex agreed, and as Julia went over to look at the old butcher's sink, Alex doused his head and body with the water and used the soap piece to clean himself. The bullet holes had closed and weren't weeping. He soaped them up. Then using the piece of rag Julia had left him, he gently rubbed the wounds and the rest of his body. Last, he soaped his wet hair and rinsed his hair and body until all the water was gone. He felt better than he had for days.

"The sink will work for clothes washing, Alex," Julia said, crossing back to him. "I'm going to get dressed and fill the water jug."

"You're not going out there by yourself, Julia," Alex said immediately. She came up to him and put her hands on his shoulders.

"Alex, we're not in Old Town now. I'm comfortable that I can handle anything that comes up here. I'll go prepared, so quit worrying."

"I don't like—" Julia stopped him with her lips. They held the kiss for a few seconds, then Julia broke the contact. She almost laughed, seeing the shock on his face.

"Just mellow out. You're not the only one that can take care of himself."

The conversation was over—that was for sure—as Julia turned away and went over to their spare clothes. She pulled on a pair of shorts and a T-shirt that wasn't too dirty. She'd been wearing the rubber sandals to wash, so she was ready to go. Julia looked around, the moonlight only helping a little. By the corner near the sink was a piece of wood. She walked over and picked it up. It was a two-foot piece of two-by-four with a bent nail in one end. She hefted it and decided it would do. Alex watched all this without saying anything. She walked over to him.

"OK, I'm ready. I'm going to go south on Mesa, back toward the restaurant. I know there was a water spigot in the back where we hid." She smiled at him.

"If I'm not back in thirty minutes, come find me."

Alex didn't like it, but he knew better than to argue with her. He had to admit it made sense. She would be much faster without him. He just glowered in his disapproval even after her quick kiss. He watched her start up the street. Only one couple was in sight, walking in the same direction she was going.

She's right, he thought. *It's much safer here.* Still, he would try to keep track of the time she was gone, and if he felt it was too long, he'd go find her. Alex went over to their makeshift bed and started sorting through the few items of spare clothing he had. It was an easy decision—one pair of pants, one pair of socks. He put the clothes on, having less trouble with the T-shirt than he expected. He'd leave the socks off for now—too hard to get them on by himself. He slid his feet into the tennis shoes. He'd leave them on in case he had to go find her, and he didn't want to walk around the shop barefoot. He was ready to go in case he had to leave quickly.

Alex stood by the doorway of the old butcher shop, watching the streets. It was still early, and other than a few cars going by, there wasn't much in the way of traffic. He spent the time leaning against the doorframe, hoping to see Julia headed back.

For her part, Julia took a more direct route, which was the one that Peter had taken them. For some reason, she felt secure here. She still scanned every nook and cranny, looking for possible danger, but so far, she hadn't seen anything. The couple walking ahead of her turned off and went up some stairs to what must be their apartment. Some of the houses had lights, and as rundown as they were, they looked inviting. Fortunately, the lack of streetlights worked in her favor, and she was able to stay unobserved as far as she knew.

She was about a block away from the Mexican restaurant, which was open for business. Julia only saw one car out front, but Peter said most of their business was from their food truck, so she wasn't surprised. She could hear strains of Spanish music as she got nearer.

Julia turned down the alley that went behind the restaurant. As she got closer, she could see the dumpster and hear voices coming through the screen door from the kitchen. With a bang, the back door opened, and a man came out with a plastic bag in his hand. Julia froze and willed herself invisible. He was wearing a stained apron and headed for the dumpster. He never looked in her direction and probably wouldn't have noticed her anyway. Intent on his task, he lifted the lid on one side of the dumpster and threw the plastic bag in. Turning quickly, we went back inside, singing a few strains of something in Spanish.

She waited a few minutes to make sure it was clear, then started making her way toward the faucet, which was ten feet from the restaurant's back door. Julia almost tripped over an old bucket but saw it just in time. She knelt down by the faucet and took the top off the quart juice bottle. Putting it under the faucet, she turned the water on, relieved when it instantly started flowing. In seconds, she filled the bottle. She turned the water off and put the cap back on the bottle. Listening intently, she stood up and started back up the alley, away from the restaurant.

The walk back to Alex was uneventful. When she was two blocks away, she could just make out an outline in the old shop's doorway. Smiling, she picked up her pace, eager to get back. By the time she got there, the doorway was empty. Alex was sitting on the cardboard bed as if he hadn't been anxiously waiting for her.

"Oh, you're back already. I forgot you were even gone." They looked at each other and laughed.

"No problems?" Alex asked.

"Not a thing," she said, gathering up the clothes and taking them to the old sink. She used a little of the water and some wadded-up newspapers to clean the sink up. After scrubbing and rinsing the clothes, she hung them on boards to air-dry. She washed Alex's socks out twice, just to be safe. When she was finished with the wash, she went over to Alex and sat down on the cardboard bed.

"I think we're ready, except for packing the clothes I just washed. I'll do that in the morning. Hopefully, they'll dry tonight."

"OK. I have a few pieces of clothing we can use for covers tonight. Better lie down. We're going to have a long journey tomorrow." Alex lay down on the cardboard, making a pillow out of his mostly empty pack. Fortunately, it was too warm for covers, which they didn't have anyway. Julia lay down next to him. She turned over on her side, facing him. The filtered moonlight caught Alex's eyes, and the whites glowed eerily.

"Have you thought about where we should head tomorrow?" she asked, knowing this was on his mind.

"I've been thinking about it. I guess we should go where we will stand out the least. We're still miles from the downtown area. That's good because our clothes will stand out and the city people probably don't like street people. Peter told us he went up there sometimes and asked for money, but I don't want to draw the attention of the police. We don't have any papers. I was thinking we could go maybe as far as West Racine and try to find a place to stay. There are still a few vacant houses that far up, but we'll have to be careful."

"Makes sense, Alex. We need to find a place to stay before trying to figure out how to make money. We're good at this part anyway. I just don't want us to get too comfortable and make mistakes that could cost us our freedom," he said.

"I don't think that's going to happen, Julia. We both know how dangerous this is. I just haven't come up with a plan to get money. We can probably steal or find enough food to get by, but at some point, we have to become part of the landscape so we fit in. I'm not much good at that part, the 'fitting in' stuff."

"We'll figure it out together, Alex."

Julia yawned, tired from the stress of the day. Alex was still wired up, probably from worrying, but he knew they both needed rest to be ready for tomorrow. He reached out and softly touched her face. She had become so important to him, but he still didn't understand how it all happened so quickly. She took his hand and kissed his palm, sending a tingle through his body. He gently pulled her face closer until their lips met.

Alex knew that if they kept kissing, things would get out of hand. As much as he wanted to explore sex with her, he knew this was the wrong time and place. He pulled back from the kiss abruptly.

"Alex, what's wrong?" she said, breathing hard.

"I want you so much, Julia, but this isn't the right place for us. I want it to be perfect."

"We're together, and it feels so good. How can it be wrong?" she said.

"I don't know. I just think this is the wrong place. You deserve better than a cardboard bed in a dirty, deserted store." He pulled his hands from her shoulders, rolling onto his side away from temptation.

Julia's body still rose and fell with her hard breathing. Then pulling herself together, she sat up and looked at him, searching his eyes for some sign of what was wrong. Finally, she spoke again. "I really don't know what just happened, Alex. Did I do something wrong?"

He sat up and pulled her to him, her firm breasts pushing into his chest. "I care more about you than my own life, Julia. You just deserve more than I can give you right now. All I ask is that you trust me when I say, as much as I want you, this is not the right place or time."

She held him tight, still not wanting to let their intimacy die.

"I do trust you, Alex," she said, pulling back so she could look into his face. "You have to know that I love you and I would die for you."

Alex didn't know what to say. He had never been in love and didn't really know what it meant. But he did know that she was the most important person in his life. Maybe that was love. He simply answered, "I would die for you too."

Chapter 28

Sleep didn't come quickly for either of them that night. The wants and needs of their bodies interfered with their rest. The next morning, as light began to break, Alex rolled off the cardboard and went to the door to look out at the street. It was quiet; no one was about yet. Alex guessed the time to be a little after 5:00 a.m.

He went over to the hanging clothes. Still a little damp, he mused, but they would dry out during the day. He slid his shorts and underwear off and replaced them with clean ones. The dampness chilled him in the cool morning air, but he soon forgot about it.

He turned and looked at Julia, who was still sleeping. She had put her shirt back on last night, and he thought she looked like an angel lying there.

As if sensing his attention, Julia opened her eyes and saw him standing by the washed clothes.

"Morning, Alex," she said, sitting up and stretching like a cat. "How did you sleep?" There was a hint of humor in her voice.

"Not so good," Alex said, coming over to her.

"Oh, something on your mind last night?" She smiled innocently.

"Nothing like that," he said in response, smiling. "Your snoring kept me awake, is all."

Julia took a swing at him, but he danced out of the way. They laughed together.

"Funny, for some reason, today seems like the start of something new," she said quizzically.

"I feel it too. Let's get our stuff together and start uptown. I'd like to get to Porfirio Diaz Street before nine and find a place to hang out."

They both got busy putting their few possessions in the backpack. They were down to one pack, which held their few bathroom items and their clothes. Julia walked over and picked up the piece of wood with the nail. She turned and looked at Alex. "Just in case."

He stretched his arms up, testing the wounds. While still red and sore, the internal damage had healed, and Alex practiced moving his arms around to stretch the tight skin.

He was healed enough to protect them if it came to it, and Julia was more than ready.

Out on the street, it was still only half-light. They started walking toward Porfirio Diaz Street, keeping an eye out for trouble. The area was visibly improving as they made their way in the direction of the city center. Still several miles from the downtown area, empty buildings were less and less prevalent and small, and local businesses were interspersed with row apartment houses. More and more cars lined the streets, probably belonging to the tenants of the row buildings. This was definitely a working-class neighborhood. To Alex, it was new territory, and he was nervous.

People were beginning to come out of their homes to go to work. Traffic was picking up, and they were seeing more and more people hurrying down the sidewalks to cars or to the bus stops. Alex and Julia were ignored. They were dressed too poorly to be of robbing value, so they were left to themselves. More and more, they saw hustlers on the street corners, beginning their day of cons and hoping to catch a tourist in the wrong part of town. Small groups of locals stood outside local grocery stores, waiting for them to open to buy cigarettes and sodas. A few looks were cast at Alex and Julia, but more interest was in Julia, even though she had dressed down and was wearing her knit cap.

At the corner of Upson Drive and Porfirio Diaz Street, a young black man stepped out of a group of four and placed himself in front of them.

"So what you doing in my neighborhood, brown boy?" he said to Alex, standing over him in a threatening manner. "You ain't from around here."

Alex stopped but kept his eyes down, not wanting to provoke him.

"Hey, I asked you a question, brown boy, and when Donny asks somebody a question, they answer me, or I feel disrespected. You don't want to disrespect Donny. Now I'll ask you again, brown boy, what you doin' in my neighborhood?"

"We're just passing through. We're not looking for trouble," Julia said, watching Alex move his feet to give him a better fighting stance. The black man didn't seem to notice.

Donny looked back at Alex.

"So what, brown boy, your girlfriend do your talking for ya? You too scared to answer Donny yourself?" He smiled, showing discolored front teeth. Alex could smell the sour stink of beer on his rancid breath. Alex knew this was going to end badly, but he wasn't one to wait, even if all he wanted was to avoid attention. He looked up at Donny, his fearless cold eyes and expressionless face making Donny pause. Julia slowly lowered the board with the nail, getting ready for what was sure to come. She had no doubt Alex would take Donny out quickly. It was the other three she was worried about. They probably have weapons, but she'd worry about that when the time came. She'd go right for the group as soon as Alex attacked Donny.

Donny sneered down at Alex. He had a good five inches and fifty pounds on the kid. He also had his friends to back him up, so this was nothing. He moved back to give himself some room. Just as he stepped back, he heard his name called out in a low voice.

"Cop, Donny, cop. Cool it, man." His three friends began melting back into the side streets. Donny saw the patrol car turn up Upson Drive toward them, and he quickly turned and walked away toward where his friends had disappeared.

"It's a patrol car, Alex," Julia said quietly, walking over to him and taking his hand. "Let's just walk up the street like nothing is wrong. They don't know we don't belong here."

They began walking up the street hand-in-hand. The patrol car pulled up alongside them, but Julia and Alex ignored it and kept walking as nonchalantly as they could. After a few seconds, the patrol car picked up speed and drove away, looking for more interesting prey. Alex and Julia stopped walking and watched it until it disappeared from sight.

They kept going block by block until they were near Lawton Drive. The houses were still mostly apartments, and the tenants were working class, which was what Alex wanted.

"We need to find a place to stay, Julia. Watch for any buildings that might work." There were still some empty buildings where businesses had failed or moved to a more lucrative area, but there were few of them. Julia saw a small corner building that must have been a barbershop or hair salon. It didn't look too bad, but it had plywood on the front window where someone had broken the glass. Discreetly, they crossed the street and walked up to it. It was getting close to eight o'clock, and the streets were busy with cars and city buses. People were walking by them as they stood by the shop front, seemingly waiting for something or someone. No one paid attention to them.

Alex tried the doorknob, but it was locked. There was also a hasp with a padlock that said "Center City Properties." He quickly looked at the hinges, but they seemed solid. Then he noticed that the plywood covering the corner window was loose, and the remaining pane of glass was held in place with duct tape.

"Julia, stand in front of me. Tell me when no one is near us." He turned back to the broken window.

"Wait, Alex."

He quickly stood up and pretended to look for a cigarette. He heard several sets of pedestrians pass by them.

"Now, Alex, you have about two minutes."

Alex turned and reached behind the plywood, working the pane of glass back and forth until the tape came loose. It fell with a loud crash.

"A guy across the street is staring at us, Alex."

He stepped up to her, turned her to face him, and kissed her deeply. His arms went around her in a close embrace. When he let her go, she was breathless and red-faced, but the man across the street had lost interest and moved on. Another group of pedestrians was walking past them, too busy with their own issues to take notice of Alex and Julia. He turned back to the window.

"Watch for me."

By pulling the plywood outward at the bottom, there was just enough room for them to crawl into the building, one at a time. The danger now was to get inside without being seen. He'd let her go first while he kept watch. He told her how to get in, and they traded places, Alex trying to shield her from view with his body. Fortunately, the next bus was not for thirty minutes, so the foot traffic was much lighter.

"Go now, Julia. Let me know when you get inside." It went without a hitch.

Inside the building, it was much nicer than most of the places they'd had to stay in before. The property company must have had it cleaned up, and unlike the deserted buildings in lower El Paso, this one hadn't been invaded by drug users and rats. It was small, with only three rooms and what looked like a small bathroom toward the back. The braces for the salon chairs were still in place, but the chairs themselves were long gone.

The first small room off the main area was once an office, and a cheap, partially broken desk was still in place. A rolling office chair was there also, but it was missing a wheel. Still, compared to where they had come from, this furniture was pretty deluxe and wouldn't have been left in the building in old El Paso. The next room was just an empty room. They didn't know what it had been used for. The last room was a storeroom. Shelves still lined the walls, waiting for the next owner. They went into the small bathroom, and it had a toilet and sink, but the water had been turned off long ago. Alex climbed up on the toilet and looked outside through the tiny window. It looked like some kind of alley that hadn't been used for a long time.

"There must be a door to that alley someplace here, Julia. Let's see if we can find it."

They went back out into the main area. Just as Alex suspected, there was a small door in the back, painted to match the walls. It was locked like the front door. He looked around for a piece of metal to use to pry the latch, but the place had been cleaned up too well. He went back into the first office and was able to break off one of the brackets on the old office desk.

"What are you going to do, Alex?" Julia asked. She had just let him do his thing, knowing he was good at this.

"I'm going to slip the latch on that door with this." He held up the broken bracket. "If we're lucky, they didn't padlock the back door."

Alex slid the bracket between the edge of the door, pushing it up against the latch of the doorknob. He worked it back and forth, pushing and pulling the door at the same time. After a few seconds, he was able to pry the latch back far enough to pull the door toward him. It opened with a screech, scraping on the floor, but it opened. The doorway went directly into the alley and had probably been used for deliveries. The alley ended just past the building, and the other end had connected to Upson Drive. Sometime in the past, the city had disconnected the alley from the street and put a curb in. Perfect for Alex and Julia, they now had a way to enter and leave without being seen.

Alex took the locking mechanism out of the door assembly. They could close the door, but it wouldn't latch. They'd use a board to lock the door from the inside. He turned to Julia, visibly pleased with himself. She smiled at him, glad to see him smile for a change.

"Looks like we're home, Julia."

Chapter 29

Over the next few weeks, Alex and Julia got to know their surroundings. Food wasn't hard to find if you didn't mind shopping in dumpsters. Alex found a water faucet at the back of a stereo shop only a block away. At night, he would fill the water jugs they had dug out of the garbage of a small drug store. They filled the toilet once a day unless it was needed more and used the bathroom sink to wash their clothes. They had to use cardboard for a bed, but they got it from behind a furniture store, and it was large sheets and clean. Julia borrowed a sheet from a clothesline, and considering their situation, they were in pretty good shape. The only real drawback was not having light at night, and they couldn't cook. Fortunately, the food they found was already cooked but cold. Greasy fish and meat were getting tiresome. Still, they'd had it much worse before.

Neither one had tried to initiate the intimate situation from the old store. For Julia, she had decided to just wait for Alex, even though her sexual urges were as strong as ever. She took pains not to undress in front of him or entice him in any way. For his part, Alex was frustrated, made worse by knowing he was the one stopping them from being lovers. Hard as it was, he still felt it was the right decision. Had Julia made advances, his resolve would have crumbled.

One night, almost three weeks after finding their new home, they lay side by side. Julia was just supposing. She'd turn to Alex and say, "Just suppose we found an old house or restaurant with electricity and water. Would we move into it?" She was always coming up with some wonderful plan where their lives suddenly got better. But Alex knew there was a real longing in these plans, and he felt he needed to find a way to make it better for her.

"I've decided that we need money," he told her one night after she told him her latest "just suppose."

"How can you do that? We're undocumented immigrants. We have no papers."

"Yes, but there are a lot of illegal aliens working in this town, so there must be a way. I'm going to find out how they do it." His mind made up, Alex rolled over on his side, his back to Julia. She lay there in the dark, thinking about what he had said. *Can he really do this?* she wondered, but then she thought of all the things they had been through just to get here. *Yes*, she mused, *he can do it*.

In the morning, Alex dressed in his best (and only) pair of long pants, washed his face and teeth, and pulled his Grateful Dead T-shirt over his head. His shoes were pretty ragged, but it couldn't be helped. Julia was still sleeping on the cardboard, and he decided not to wake her. He went out the back door, hoping she would wake soon and put the door locking board in place. Julia listened to him leave, silently wishing him all the luck in the world. She got up, locked the door and went in to do her morning wash.

Alex was four blocks away, near a construction site where they were building something big. The workers must have been on a break because several of them were sitting by a bulldozer, smoking. They looked Spanish, and Alex went up to them and said, "Buenos dias, amigos."

They looked at him suspiciously.

"Soy nuevo en la ciudad y me preguntaba si había puestos de trabajo aquí?" Alex asked them if there were any jobs here.

They looked at each other. One of them, the biggest of the group, put his cigarette out and stood up. He walked over to Alex.

"Quién es usted?" he said. ("Who are you?")

"Mi nombre es Alex y yo soy nuevo en la ciudad. Estoy tratando de encontrar trabajo." ("My name is Alex, and I'm new to the city. I'm looking for work.")

"Hacer los papellas?" he asked Alex. ("Do you have papers?")

"No," Alex replied.

"*Ay stupido*, you never admit that to anyone. Always say, 'Yes, of course, I have papers,' even if it isn't true. Boy, you must be new here, or you'd already be on the bus back to Mexico." He turned back to his friends.

"Probably just came in from the country." They laughed at Alex, but he could tell they meant him no harm.

"I need to find some work so I can get a place with running water and electricity."

"That's all you need, running water and electricity?" They all thought this was hysterical. Alex didn't get the joke.

"Come, we'll help you get your water and electricity. Pablo got picked up last night, and we are short one crew. It's hard work and pays little, but it is a job."

Alex worked three hours that day and forty-four eight-hour days straight after that. Of course, they gave him the dirtiest and hardest jobs in the beginning. He and Julia lived in the old salon, not spending any money and saving for an apartment of their own. They were excited. Neither really thought this could happen.

Alex learned a lot from Frank and the other Mexican workers. They worked hard, mostly doing the labor jobs that the Americans were too important or too lazy to do. Alex didn't care; he was working toward their dream. When he got back at night, he'd find Julia had his dinner waiting, sometimes even store-bought food. His clothes would be washed and his bed ready. For the first two weeks, he could barely stay awake until dinner was over because he was so tired and sore, but after a while, he got used to the long hours and hard work. One rule Julia had was that as soon as he got home, he would get a bath, which amounted to him standing in a metal pan while Julia poured cold water on him. He'd soap up. Then she would rinse him off. At first, she helped him wash, but they soon saw where that was going, so now she just poured water on him and laughed as he howled. On the forty-fourth day, Alex showed up for work, but Frank met him at the fence.

"Go home, Alex, no work today. I'm the only one working. I found out ICE is doing a spot check today, so you don't want to be here. Check with me tomorrow to see if it's clear."

"How did you know they were coming? I thought they did surprise inspections."

Frank smiled. "They do, but one of the inspectors is a relative of mine. Go home." Alex did as Frank said.

Julia was surprised to see him home, but he explained about the inspectors.

"You're lucky he's taking care of you, Alex."

"I know. I would never let them send me to Mexico." He put his arms around her and held her close. Pulling away suddenly, he exclaimed, "I know, let's go look for a place to live. How much have we saved up?"

Shocked, Julia stammered, "I don't know. We'll have to count it." They went into the room with the shelves, and Alex pried out the loose board in the corner of the floor. Inside was a coffee can with a lid. Pulling it out, he took off the plastic lid and dumped the cash on the floor. There was just over three thousand dollars in folded-up bills.

"I've never seen so much money," he said in awe. He picked up a piece of paper that was with the cash. It said, "Borrow four dollars for soap and woman stuff, Julia."

"I'm sorry, Alex, I needed the soap for your baths, and well, I needed the woman things for me. I'll pay you back."

Alex looked at her quizzically. "This money is as much yours as it is mine. You have every right to spend our money. Take anything you want."

Julia's eyes teared up. "But I know you work so hard, and I do nothing."

Alex put the money down and reached out to touch her face. "Everything I do is for you, Julia." He drew her to him and softly kissed her lips.

She smiled, but they decided to put off hunting for an apartment for a while. The sit-ups pulled at his wounds, but Alex worked through the pain. He had to get back in shape for their move uptown. While the streets would be much less dangerous than in Old Town, their safety could not be guaranteed unless he was healed 100 percent.

He managed to do a hundred sit-ups, but that was much less than before he got hurt. He probed the wrinkled skin around the bullet wounds. The scar tissue was hard, but underneath the hard skin, it was still tender when he pressed on the scars. *These minor discomforts are a lot better than just a week ago,* Alex thought to himself. He started doing squat thrusts, an exercise that did not aggravate the wounds. After fifteen minutes, he was shaky but not too bad. He didn't bother with chin-ups or push-ups; both would be too hard on him. However, he found two old gallon paint cans that were empty, so he filled them with broken concrete. He guessed their weight to be around twenty pounds each. Using the handles, he did fifty curls with each arm, bending from the elbow down. Alex was drenched in sweat when he finished, but he was satisfied for now. Tomorrow he'd do better. He thought he might start running too.

Alex had been back to work for the past eight days. No more surprise inspections; they had moved on to other contractors with Latino workers. On the way home from work, Alex made a decision. He would take the next day off, and he and Julia would go apartment hunting. The idea scared him, but it was Julia's dream, so he'd help her find it.

Today was the tenth of September. He and Julia had been living near Upson Drive for the past ninety days. His job was almost over, the construction project mostly finished. Even though they had made a home in the old building, Alex was eager to find a real home for Julia and more permanent work. He was still not sure what his true goal was, but now his days were filled with hard labor and getting by. He knew there was more to life than just getting by.

He and Julia sometimes talked about their dreams. Hers were mostly centered on stability, while his were just undefined. Soon they would move—he knew that—but what else was to happen? He didn't know.

Chapter 30

Alex and Julia left early. They walked east on Fewel Street toward Mundy Drive and the park. Even though the Chihuahuita area was not known as an upscale neighborhood in El Paso, to them, the obvious well-to-do neighborhoods were intimidating compared to where they were from. Alex was nervous, not used to blocks of houses without broken windows or boarded-up doors. Many of the driveways had cars that looked like they ran. It was a working-class neighborhood without any frills, but lights glowed in windows in the early morning dawn. A few of the buildings had vacancy signs in windows or on stakes stuck in the dead grass. They looked at each building, searching for signs that said the manager was on site. Neither had a cell phone and no way to call the numbers listed on most of the vacancy signs. They finally found one on Fewel Street, not far from the park.

"It looks too nice, Julia. I doubt we could afford something like this," Alex said. It was a duplex, rundown by most standards, with dead grass in front and no backyard. But the windows all had glass, and old sheets had been hung up for drapes so they couldn't see inside.

"It won't hurt to ask, though. Come on, let's at least look inside." Julia went to the rented side of the duplex and knocked on the door. A young girl came to the door and asked Julia what she wanted.

"We'd like to look at the apartment next door," Julia told her.

"Go ahead. It's not locked. My mom isn't home now, but if you like it, you can come back later and talk to her." She abruptly closed the door.

Alex had stayed back from the entrance and waited for Julia to return. He watched her coming back from the door.

"Let's go look at the apartment," she said smiling, taking his hand and pulling him toward the front door of the unit.

"They gave you the key?" he said curiously.

"No, she said it is unlocked, and if we like it, we can come back and talk to them."

"Did she say how much it is?"

"No, we'll have to ask when we come back—I mean, *if* we come back."

They walked up to the front door, and when Julia turned the doorknob, it opened right up. They stepped in and looked around, noticing the dust and clutter on the old hardwood floors of the living room. Julia went to the kitchen, marveling at the old electric stove and oven and the refrigerator that had seen better days. There was no electricity, so she couldn't test to see if they worked. She went over to the old double sink and turned the faucets on. Both hot and cold water worked, but of course, the water didn't get hot.

Alex had gone down the narrow hallway to the first bedroom. It had an old double bed with a stained-up mattress. Two desk lamps sat atop a chest of drawers with missing handles. Another old sheet covered the window for privacy. He left the room and continued to the bathroom between the two bedrooms. The bathroom was actually in fair condition. The tub/shower was cracked and chipped, but it looked usable. The showerhead was there, and the drain looked functional. Alex tried the faucets, and they ran water. The mirror above the sink was cracked, and the countertop was discolored, but it all looked like it would work.

He left the bathroom for the last bedroom. This one had two windows that were covered by sheets, but that was all. He heard Julia come up behind him and watched her examine the room. When she looked at him, she had tears in her eyes.

"I love it," she said tearfully.

Alex looked at her for a minute, then said, "If you're sure, then we need to come back when the owner is here." She nodded yes, and they turned away from the room and went back up the hallway toward the front door. She slipped her hand into his, reconfirming her decision.

Outside, Alex closed the front door, leaving it unlocked like it was when they got there. As he turned away, he heard a car pull up the driveway to the other unit. A harried-looking woman pushed the driver's door open and climbed out of the battered Ford. She straightened and looked over at them. Her expression was guarded.

"Can I help you with something?" she called out, not moving away from her car.

"Yes, ma'am," Alex replied. "Your daughter said we could look at the empty unit, and we'd like to talk to you about it." He didn't move toward her; he'd wait until she invited him. The woman took her time looking him over, then Julia.

"Well, I got a few questions for you before we talk renting. Come over here, and we can talk." She turned back to the old Ford, opened the back door, and took out a brown bag of what looked like groceries. She closed the door and put the bag on the hood of the car. As Alex and Julia came closer, she looked them over again, noticing the worn but clean clothes. The boy couldn't be more than sixteen years old, the girl not much older. She knew street kids grew up fast, so age didn't always mean much.

"I don't abide no drug using here—that a problem with you?"

Both Alex and Julia said it wasn't a problem.

"You got jobs? I can't afford no charity cases."

"Yes, ma'am," Alex said. "I work for Johnson Construction over on Fifth Street."

"How about you, girl? You work too?"

"No, ma'am," Julia said shyly. "I stay home and take care of the house."

"Well, I guess that's OK long as you two can pay the rent. You work construction, huh? Handy with tools?" she said, turning her attention back to Alex. "If we work a deal, I might be able to use some help fixing a few things here. Be willing to take a little off the rent. Hey, you got papers, right? I don't need no trouble with Immigration."

Remembering what Frank had said, Alex replied, "Yes, ma'am, we got papers. We'll be no problem for you."

Julia didn't say anything.

"Well, you two look OK, but I won't put up with any problems from you. I charge $650 a month, and you pay for water and electricity. I want a month's rent up front, and I'll waive the deposit if you help me hook up a new water heater in the unit. The old one started leaking a month ago, and the old renter never told me. By the time I found out, it was too late. The new heater ain't really new. My brother gave it to me, but he says it works, and I can't afford to be choosy."

"Sure, ma'am, be glad to help, but I can't do it till this weekend. That OK?"

"Yeah," she said, "that's OK. When do you want to move in? We gotta put the hot water in first—that's the law."

"If I get the hot water fixed Saturday, could we move in then?" Alex asked, knowing Julia would be nervous and afraid that they wouldn't get it for some reason, so the sooner they could move in, the better.

"Well, I guess so. Sure could use the money. Hey, how do I know you'll be back Saturday? Maybe I need some kind of deposit or something."

"How about $50 until Saturday. Will that hold it?"

"Guess that's OK," she said.

Julia counted $50 from the stack of bills in her pocket.

"Are you sure you're not drug dealers? How come you carry around so much money?" she said suspiciously.

"We don't have a bank account and have no other safe place to keep the money," Alex said quickly.

She was silent for a minute. "I don't trust them banks neither, but you gotta be careful carrying money like that around here. Best you just keep it in your pocket out of sight. Name's Louise Sojun, by the way. Ain't much on paperwork, so we'll shake hands to seal the deal." She put out her right hand, and Alex took it in his and gave it a shake. Then Julia did the same.

"OK, I'll see you two on Saturday." She turned back to her bag of groceries, picked it up off the hood of the car, and walked up the path to her door.

Julia was anxious and nervous and kept saying she knew the apartment would be gone by Saturday. Alex just ignored her misgivings. They had made a deal and shook hands, which was the end of it for Alex. He had little experience with deals or contracts, but a promise to him was as ironclad as any piece of paper. He would learn better as he got older.

Saturday morning, Julia was up and dressed before 6:00 a.m.

"Julia, it's too early to go there. Just relax a little while." He patted the bed beside him.

"I can't, Alex. I'm too nervous. We need to be ready to leave, so please get up and get dressed."

Alex knew there would be no reasoning with her, so he sighed, got out of bed, and went to wash up in the bowl. Having cleaned up as best as he could, he got dressed and went over to where she paced.

"OK, it's about seven, be near eight, by the time we walk there. I've got my tool bag, so let's go."

"Julia let out a little squeal and went out the door, barely managing not to run."

"Relax, Julia. It's gonna be a long day." Reluctantly, she slowed her pace to match his.

Chapter 31

It was a beautiful Saturday morning. The sun was warm, even this early. No hint of the approaching winter coolness, and this just fed Julia's excitement even more. As they made their way toward the duplex, she chattered to Alex about unimportant things like the squirrels and birds just to keep her mind calm. Finally, they rounded the corner, and there it was. Anxiously, Julia went up to the landlord's door and quietly knocked.

"Nice and early, I like that. Looks like your husband is ready to work, too. I see he has a tool belt. You got the rent?"

Julia nodded yes.

"Well, OK, give me a minute, and I'll meet you next door. Go on over."

Eagerly, Julia did as she was told, dragging Alex along with her. As soon as they were inside, Julia left Alex to make her plans to upgrade the rooms. Alex went into the laundry room, where the replacement water heater sat. The old water heater had been removed by the landlord's brother, and a mess of pipes and wires stuck out of the wall.

Alex looked at the connections, pleased to see that both the replacement water heater and the existing pipes had the connectors he needed. This should be an easy project.

Connecting the water pipes went well after Alex had wrestled the new water heater in place. The 220-volt connection wasn't quite as easy. The wires coming out from the junction box were too short to reach the new heater connections, so he had to splice some wire together to make it reach. After he tightened everything down, he used a thin layer of electrical tape to insulate his connections. He'd gotten the Teflon and electrical tape from his job site after asking permission to take it. Once everything was hooked up, he turned on the cold water to begin filling the tank. He could hear the water rushing in and didn't see any leaks. So far, so good. He waited a few minutes until he figured the water was above the heating elements and flipped the breaker on. No sparks, so hopefully, all was good.

Meanwhile, Julia had paced off the window sizes for curtains and went through each room measuring. She had brought a piece of blank paper and a pencil and drew pictures of what she wanted to do in each room. She tested the stove in the kitchen, and it worked. When she opened the refrigerator, a sour smell emerged from the remains of rotting food left inside, but the light came on. When she turned the thermostat on, she heard the compressor kick in.

Alex joined her in the kitchen. "How's it going?" he asked.

"Oh, Alex, I'm so excited. I have so many ideas on how to fix it up."

Just then, the front door opened, and the landlady came in.

"Sorry it took me so long. My daughter wanted to talk. You about ready to start installing the water heater?"

"Actually, it's done. Let's see if it's getting hot yet."

Alex walked over to the kitchen sink and turned the tap on. It ran cold for a few seconds, and then warm water came spilling out.

"Seems to be working," Alex told her.

"Hmm," the landlady said. "Let me go look at what you did." She went into the laundry room and came back out a few seconds later.

"Looks like a real professional job. How'd you do it so fast?"

"It wasn't a hard job," Alex said.

"Well, if you have the rent, I guess the place is yours."

Julia walked over and gave her the money.

"I might have other jobs like that if you want that kind of work. It's hard to find someone to do this stuff at a reasonable price."

"I'd be interested," Alex replied.

"I'll leave you to your moving then. Good luck with your new place." She turned and went out the door.

Alex watched her leave and felt a hand slide into his. Julia said, "Thank you, Alex," and gently kissed him on the lips. Tears glistened in her eyes.

Embarrassed, Alex said, "Let's get moving then. I'd like to spend the night in our new house." He started out the door and stopped. Turning back to her, he said, "Would you ask the landlady for the key when you see her next?" He went out the door, heading up the street toward their old building.

Julia loved their new apartment. Alex had been working long hours as his job wound down and worked with the landlady in his spare time. They spent money carefully, fixing up their home as cheaply as possible. Mostly, this fell on Julia, with Alex so busy working most of the time. But it was coming along. She found ways to get things they needed from the community—old furniture, drapes, even a broken washing machine that Alex fixed for her. She was happy and content, but she could sense the restlessness in Alex. There wasn't much she could do about that. She brought home an old television, and he made an antenna from instructions he found in an old, discarded book. When they turned it on, Alex watched it for a few minutes and kept changing channels as if looking for something specific. She didn't know what he was searching for, and he wouldn't say. He quickly lost interest in the TV and wandered back into the bedroom to read one of the discarded books he had brought home. His reading and writing skills had improved and were even better than hers now.

Chapter 32

As the days passed, Alex became more and more remote and withdrawn. Julia tried to talk to him, but he wasn't responsive. He was still even-tempered and always did what she asked him to do, but it was him she wanted, not his skills. Finally, one night she decided it was time to force him to talk to her. They had just gone to bed and turned out the light when Julia turned to face him in the dark.

"Alex, I need to know what is going on. You won't talk to me about what's bothering you, and I'm tired of guessing. I need to know if you want me to leave. I don't feel welcome here anymore."

She felt him turn toward her in the dark, but he was still silent.

"Alex, I . . ."

Then he answered. "I don't know what we're going to do when my job ends. I don't make enough money doing repairs, and we have rent and utilities to pay for. I don't want to lose this house. I know how much you love it, and I don't want to disappoint you." She heard him sigh.

"You should know better, Alex," she said in a stern voice. "I'm not here with you for the house or your money. I'm here because we belong together." Then more softly, she continued, "We can lose everything, and I'll still be happy as long as we are together." She reached out and took his hand. "You are everything to me."

Alex moved and put his arms around her. He held her tightly, and she held him back. He spoke quietly into her neck.

"I want the world for you, but I can't give it to you."

"Just hold me like this, and I'll have everything I've ever wanted."

She gently raised his face from her neck and kissed him. "Tomorrow, you and I will figure out our future, but tonight, we are all that matters."

She moved away from him, and he could hear the rustle of clothing. When she lay back down next to him, he quickly realized she was naked.

"Julia, I . . ." But she shushed him with her lips and tongue.

"Take off your clothes, Alex," she said quietly and reached over to untie his pajama pants. Both exhausted and fulfilled, they lay together in the warm night, marveling at this wonderful new experience. Not wanting to break the magic spell, they drifted off to sleep without worry or concern.

In the morning, Alex quietly got out of bed, trying not to wake Julia. They were both still naked, and he marveled at her beautiful brown skin against the white sheets. Julia opened her eyes slowly and saw him staring at her. She didn't try to cover herself, pleased with his approval. She reached up to pull him back into bed, but he resisted, even as his body reacted to the sight of her.

"I have to leave for work. I've overslept, but I can still be on time if I leave soon."

"I suggest you take a shower first," she said with a grin, stretching languorously and purposely making him more uncomfortable.

Forcing his eyes away, he went into the bathroom and quickly showered and dressed. When he came back out, she was under the covers, fading back to sleep. He went into the kitchen and made a sandwich, grabbed an apple, and filled his lunchbox. He filled the old thermos he had found with tap water. Alex went back to their bedroom and said goodbye from the doorway. Julia's eyes opened, and she said she'd be waiting for him to come home. He turned and left quickly, embarrassed by his inappropriate thoughts.

When Alex got to work, the Johnson Construction Company manager's van was parked by the foreman's trailer. Alex wondered why the manager was here so early. He usually just came by for the monthly inspections or when he had questions for Frank, who had been made production manager. The door to the trailer was open when he walked by, and the two men were sitting by the old desk talking. Frank saw him and waved him over. Aware of his beat-up thermos and lunchbox, Alex was nervous at being singled out.

Maybe this is my last day, he thought as he had many times before over the last two years. Alex entered the trailer and walked up to them. The two men looked at Alex as if trying to make up their minds about something.

"Sit down, Alex. We'd like to talk to you." He pointed at a folding chair by the desk, and Alex sat, not saying anything to the two men.

"Alex, this is Martin Frazer, general manager of Johnson Construction."

The other man nodded to Alex and offered him his hand. Alex leaned over and took it, and they shook briefly.

"Mr. Frazer here has a unique problem. Maybe you'd like to explain it to Alex, Martin."

"Alex, our company employs more than a thousand Mexican—ahhh, *legal* immigrants like yourself. We have construction contracts all over the state of Texas as well as New Mexico and Arizona. While these employees are excellent workers and very affordable, they do present a few problems for our company. Sometimes, because they come from a country that has different labor laws than we do, their paperwork isn't quite what the US is looking for. Johnson Construction has decided that we need a department that specializes in helping them get the proper documentation. The trouble with that idea is that management in our company is all US-based and doesn't really understand some of the issues the immigrants are facing. Because of that, we've decided to create a new position, sort of a liaison or agent that can help us better understand their needs and ours." He stopped talking and stood up. Walking over to the window, he continued talking with his back to Alex.

"Frank has been with the company for more than ten years, and since he has been dealing with the immigrant workers daily, we've decided to let him run this new department. I'm happy to say that Frank has accepted the position, but he had a condition. Frank feels that with this job site finishing soon, he'd rather keep you as a resource than lose you and has asked that you join him in the new department. So, Alex, we'd like to offer you the position of assistant to the manager, Foreign Personnel Department. Of course, there will be a substantial pay raise, and the department will stay here in Texas, so you won't have to move. You'll get training about our corporate structure, rules, and regulations so you can better understand our needs. I understand that some of your immigration paperwork got lost, so one of our first tasks is to make sure you comply with US regulations. Not a problem—we have a lot of friends in Washington, DC."

He stopped talking and turned to look at Alex. "I know this is a lot to digest, so why don't you take a day or two off to think about it?"

"With full pay, of course," Frank said quickly, smiling at the general manager.

Frazer turned to Frank and smiled, then turned back to Alex. "Of course, it's paid time off." Then he turned back to face Frank. "Frank, I need to get back to the office, so I'll wish you boys a good day." He shook their hands again, then turned and went out the door. Over his shoulder, he said, "And, Alex, I hope you say yes."

Frank and Alex were silent when Martin Frazer left—both lost in thought.

"The thing is, Alex, you can help a lot of your countrymen in this new job," Frank said suddenly.

"But, Frank," Alex said, "I'm only nineteen and don't have the education for this. I don't know if the guys will listen to someone as young as me, so I'm not sure I can do the job."

"Alex, you've worked with these men for the last two years, and they trust you and come to you for advice. Your age doesn't seem to matter to them. I have faith in you, Alex, and I'll be right there to help," Frank said. "I wouldn't have asked for you if I didn't think you could do the job. Just take some time and think about it. It's really a great opportunity for both of us." He started shuffling the papers on his desk, so Alex knew the conversation was over. Alex got up out of his chair and went out the door, heading home to find Julia.

Chapter 33

Ramon came into the office slowly. He was worried about this meeting. They must have found out he was undocumented, he thought as he waited to be shown in. When the office manager brought Ramon to Alex Lima's office, he was surprised at how young he was. He looked to be in his early twenties, about the age of Ramon's son. But he was a powerful man in this company, regardless of his age, and Ramon desperately wanted to keep his job. Mr. Lima had a reputation for fairness, so maybe Ramon would be OK. If he called ICE on Ramon, he'd be arrested and deported back to Mexico. His family would suffer because he'd have no income, and there were no prospects for work in his town. Even though he only earned minimum wage now, it was much more than he could earn in Mexico, but that was a moot point since there were no jobs there for him anyway.

Alex motioned for him to come in and close the door. He pointed to the chair in front of his desk, and Ramon sat down. Alex spoke to him in Spanish, which was good because Ramon had poor English skills.

"Ramon, I am Alex Lima. How are you today?" He stood up and put his hand out to Ramon, and he shook it tentatively. Ramon noticed there was something about his eyes. They looked old in his young face, as if he had seen more of life than his years could account for. Alex sat back down and picked up some papers on his desk.

"I understand you have been with us for two years working on the Dallas Mall project. Is this correct?"

"Yes, s-sir," Ramon stammered, sweat beginning to collect on his scalp.

"Roberto Pina is your supervisor?"

"Yes, sir," Ramon answered, wondering how far he would get if he made a run for it.

"Mr. Pina says you're a good worker and an honest man, Ramon. Our company tries to help our good workers, and I am here to see how we can help you, Ramon." They talked for another thirty minutes. After Ramon left, Alex had his secretary take the sponsorship paperwork to the County Courthouse to begin the immigration permit process. With Johnson Construction sponsoring Ramon, the approval would be swift unless some type of legal issue showed up on his background check. It wouldn't, Alex knew, since they had already run the check on Ramon.

Alex was finished for the day. He was excited to get home to Julia. He put his coat on, and like every day before he left the office, he picked up the glass paperweight with the three marbles inside and stared at it for a few minutes. His father said the marbles represented something important and that someday, Alex would understand what that meant, but that day hadn't come yet. For the past nineteen years, ever since he was a child living on the streets of old El Paso, he had wondered why his father had disappeared and even if he was still alive. Somehow, someday, he would find out what had happened to his father.

Alex said goodnight to the office manager and left the building. Even though his house was close enough to walk to, he usually drove to work so he could run errands and drive to the construction sites. He unlocked his car and took off his jacket before getting in. He threw it on the passenger seat, started the car, and looked around before backing out of his parking spot. He didn't see any cars nearby, so he backed out and turned to drive out of the fenced lot. He didn't notice the man in the car parked on the other side of the fence watching him leave.

That night, Julia surprised him by asking, "Do you ever think about having kids, Alex?"

"Uhm," he stammered, blushing. "I guess I don't think that far ahead."

"Alex, I want to get married. We have legal status, a good income, and we both know we'll never leave each other." Julia stopped talking, watching the expression on Alex's face. "I want a family of our own, Alex. You'll make a great father, and I think I'll be a good mother," she continued.

They were married by the Justice of the Peace two days later. Frank was their witness.

Chapter 34

Alex turned the car down Fewel Street toward their duplex. A gray Toyota Camry followed a block behind. Alex pulled into his driveway, parking in front of his door. The duplex was still as shabby-looking as when they rented it, but Alex didn't notice. Inside, Julia had made it comfortable, and that's what mattered to him. He was twenty-four, and even though he made enough money for them to move to a better neighborhood, neither he nor Julia really cared about that. Maybe when the kids were older, they'd find a house with a yard and good schools, but for now, this was fine.

Alex got out of the car and went up to the door and knocked. As was their rule, the door was locked, and although Alex had a key, he liked it when Julia met him at the door. He heard the door unlock, and he pulled the door open. Julia was standing there, radiant as always, with an arm full of a squirming Carlos. A wide smile was on his face as he saw his dad. At one year old, he was already a master of displaying his approval or displeasure, whichever happened to be on his agenda at that time. His approval was obvious as he reached out for Alex to hold him. Alex turned to close the door, subconsciously noticing the gray car driving slowly past their house.

Julia handed him to Alex, saying, "Tag, you're it. I'm going to the kitchen to make dinner. Juan is in his room, playing with the computer." She blew him a kiss and disappeared.

Alex and Carlos went down the hallway to the boys' room. Julia had decorated it with bright colors that matched the bedspreads on their bunk beds. Seeing some of his favorite toys on the carpet, Carlos indicated he wanted down, pointing at them. Alex put him down, and Carlos held onto his leg. He let go and took a few unstable steps, then landed on his butt. He decided crawling was safer and made his way over to the block set. Juan was still pecking away at the keyboard, so Alex went over to his oldest son.

"Dad, did you know that pterodactyls were reptiles, not birds? They were, like, flying dinosaurs. Isn't that cool?" His three-year-old eyes glowed with excitement. As always, Alex marveled at his vocabulary. Alex didn't have his language skills when he was three. Juan was also bilingual, equally proficient in Spanish, and even Carlos could speak gibberish in either language. He marveled at how much Julia's love of reading books had influenced both children. The nightly bedtime readings had profoundly affected their learning abilities. Alex couldn't be prouder.

On Saturday, Alex woke up when Julia got out of bed. As usual, Carlos was softly snoring where his mom had been. He could hear Julia in the kitchen, making coffee with her new Nespresso machine. She loved the coffee maker, spending a small fortune on coffee pods for it. He listened as the machine sounded like a jet taking off, then went silent as it finished its process. She brought a cup into the bedroom for Alex.

He sat in bed with Carlos, sipping his coffee and just enjoying the unhurried morning. He finished the coffee and put the empty cup on the nightstand, then got up and went to the dresser, looking for socks and a T-shirt. As he did almost every day for the past four years, he was preparing to run his five miles, then come back and do his exercises.

Julia came back to the room and took his place sitting on the bed. She'd read and sip her coffee until one (or both) of the boys woke up. Seeing that Alex had his shoes on and was ready to go out, she got off the bed and kissed him. Alex kissed her back.

"Be careful and hurry back. It's pancake Saturday, you know."

Alex groaned. Julia's pancakes could be measured in pounds, but the boys loved them, so that was good enough. He'd have to do twice as many exercises today after eating them. He told her goodbye and went to the front door, unlocked it, and went outside. He stood on the porch until he heard Julia lock the door behind him. A gray car drove by and triggered a thought in Alex's mind. He had seen that car before, and as he thought about it, one looking like that was parked across from his office when he left work the other day. Of course, it was a very common color and model, and he was probably just being paranoid. There was no reason to think that anyone was watching him. Still, old habits die hard, and it stayed in the back of his mind as he ran across town.

Chapter 35

Raul turned the corner on Center Street and pulled the Camry over to the curb. He took a quick look around, making sure no one was nearby. He reached under the newspaper on the passenger seat and slid the gun onto his lap. It was a Glock 40, well oiled and untraceable. It was a gun he had taken from a cop after he shot him. Tracking the gun would get the police nowhere.

He pulled the slide open, loading a shell into the chamber. He closed the slide, released the hammer back down and put on the safety. He put it back under the newspaper on the passenger seat.

Raul sat there for a few minutes, planning his next moves. It had taken him four years to track down Alex and Julia, mostly because nobody knew their last names. He got lucky when one of his guys was selling dope to some workers at Johnson Construction, and Alex's name came up. They mentioned how young he was, especially for being in management. Raul had one of his police connections run a check on Alex Lima, and it came back pretty much empty. It seemed his life didn't start until four years ago.

The age was right, and that was enough for Raul to get Anson up here to ID him. Anson agreed—it was the Alex he was looking for.

Raul had watched him for the past two weeks. He'd seen the girl Julia and quickly found out where they lived. Having identified both of them and their two kids, it was now just time to plan how he would take them all out. There was no question in Raul's mind that Alex was the one who had killed his brother.

Raul was a careful man. Even with his "friends" in law enforcement, there were plenty of people who wanted him dead. That was just part of being on top in the drug business. That's why he was sitting here planning how to take them out instead of rushing in. He wasn't afraid of Alex—after all, the guy worked a desk job. Besides, Raul had faced plenty of men that were more of a threat than this guy. Still, he didn't want to make a scene, so he'd do it quick and easy, probably in the guy's home. Besides, he wanted to kill the wife and kids at the same time. That message would get out to his enemies and help keep them at bay.

Alex had just gotten back from his run. He decided to shower and eat breakfast before doing his exercises. Stepping out of the shower, he put on a fresh T-shirt and shorts and went into the dining room, where noises of approval were coming from the boys. He watched from the hallway as Juan squeezed syrup on his stack of pancakes. Carlos was impatiently waiting for his turn with the syrup. *Hopefully, Julia will help him*, thought Alex, remembering previous episodes of Carlos and the syrup bottle. Sure enough, Julia took the syrup bottle from Juan and "helped" Carlos put a nice gooey layer of syrup on his pancakes. Then she put the bottle down out of his reach and cut the pancakes into bite-size chunks. Juan needed no help and was attacking his stack with gusto. Alex figured it was safe to come in now that Carlos was disarmed.

He sat in front of a pile of pancakes, making appreciative noises to keep Julia happy. He put his own syrup on and began eating. Julia and Carlos shared his meal. She was still nursing him, and she knew he wasn't really hungry, but he loved to eat with everyone. They took turns forking bites into their mouth. Sometimes Carlos even got the pancakes into his mouth. Typical happy, loud, and messy Saturday morning at the breakfast table. Alex and Julia loved every minute of it.

Chapter 36

Raul had watched Alex for two weeks straight, so he knew about the morning runs. Although it would be much simpler to take Alex out with a drive-by during his run, he still preferred killing him at the house while they were all together. No loose ends.

He turned on the ignition, and the Camry started right up. He checked his mirrors and pulled out into the street, headed toward the duplex. He was sure Alex would be back from the run by now.

He pulled over to the curb about five blocks from the duplex. Sliding the gun onto his lap, he took a four-inch silencer out of his pocket and started screwing it onto the barrel of the Glock. Since he was going to do this in broad daylight, he needed to be as inconspicuous as possible, so there should be no loud noises like gunshots. He didn't bother to put the gun back under the paper, just let it lie in his lap. Raul figured he should go another few blocks, then park the car, and continue on foot. He'd stick the gun in his waistband under the jacket.

Pulling out, he didn't notice the police car about a block behind him. He drove slowly up Fewel Street, looking for a good spot to park. Lights flashed in his rear-view mirror, and he looked up and saw the police car.

"Shit," he muttered. He was only driving about fifteen miles per hour, and the cop was flashing him to speed up.

Raul realized he'd have to do the hit some other time since he'd been made. He accelerated gently to thirty-five, the police car right behind him. He knew that if they pulled him over, he'd have to kill them both. He reached down with his right hand, gripping the pistol. The police car suddenly turned right and sped away, apparently answering a call. Raul breathed a sigh of relief but kept driving away from Alex's house. He'd have to come back after dark when things were quiet. He had noticed the empty lot at the back of their apartment and figured that was how he would approach it.

Oblivious to what had just happened, Alex and his family were having a relaxing Saturday. Even though Alex had an important job in the company, he never brought his work home with him. He had much more important things to think about when he was home.

They planned to go to the park that afternoon with Mrs. Sojun and her daughter. The landlady and her daughter had become unofficial family members, Mrs. Sojun being *ama* (grandma) to the boys and her daughter Rachael, *tia* (auntie). Mrs. Sojun always let them know that she and Rachael were available to babysit if Julia and Alex wanted to go out. They hadn't taken her up on it yet.

So many changes had taken place since Alex and Julia ran away from old El Paso. Alex never thought he would be working uptown, let alone in a management position. But then, neither of them ever considered that four short years after leaving, they'd be married with two children.

Alex and Julia had talked about picking up his mother's body. He would like to bury her properly, and Julia agreed. However, both knew this was not the proper time if someone was watching them. Maybe in the near future, there would be a time.

Saturday at the park was great. Both boys ran—well, Juan ran, while Carlos mostly crawled. There were slides and a sandbox, and Carlos crawled across the grass to the sandbox to dig holes. Juan went to the slides and climbed up, sliding down and squealing in pleasure. Tired of the slides, he went looking for something more interesting like the hobby horses or maybe the spinner if someone would spin it for him.

Alex got up and went over to the spinner. "Hop on, Juan. I'll give you a ride."

Juan climbed up on the ride and hung onto the metal rails. When Alex saw that he was ready and holding on tight, he spun the ride, watching to make sure Juan was holding on tight. He screamed with delight, spinning around at a good clip. Alex kept it going a few seconds longer, then stopped pushing and let the ride slow itself down.

They spent about two hours at the park, hopefully wearing the boys out enough for a nap at home. They packed up their drinks and leftover snacks. Mrs. Sojun picked Carlos up, and they all headed back to the car.

Back at the duplex, the boys washed up and, with Julia urging them, headed for their room for a nap. Juan believed he was too old for naps, but as soon as his head hit the pillow, he was out. Carlos wasn't far behind.

Closing their door softly, Julia went back to the living room and sat down next to Alex. He was reading a paperback he'd picked up somewhere and looked completely relaxed. Julia sat next to him and slowly drifted off, comfortable in their cozy little house.

Chapter 37

Sunday morning, Alex was up early, hoping to get his run in before the rest of the house woke up. He downed a quick cup of coffee and headed out of the house, the sun just starting to brighten the day.

Alex turned down Fewel Street. Crossing the street, he ran up Comwell Avenue. He crossed again at the stop sign, noticing how little traffic was out this time of the morning. Most folks slept in on Sunday, which made these morning runs much more enjoyable. He ran by the old construction site where he got his first job, now a full-blown shopping mall. All the while, he was subconsciously watching for a gray car, but it was nowhere to be seen.

Raul woke at about eight o'clock. The prostitute was long gone; he never let them sleep over. He lay there, thinking about where to go for breakfast. He'd plan the day over hot coffee and grits.

He took a quick shower and, as was his routine, checked his messages on his iPhone. He had the usuals. His captain was letting him know that their guys were in place, even though the drug trade wouldn't really begin for hours. Raul liked his guys to be ready for the all-nighters or early birds. If his dealers had to sit on a corner a little longer than the other distributors, hey, that was just business. Raul didn't get to the top of the food chain by missing opportunities.

Alex got back home and softly knocked on the door. Julia let him in, telling him to be quiet because the boys were still out. Alex smiled and said he might have another cup of coffee. She was surprised; he was a one-cup coffee drinker normally. She went back to the boys' room, opening their door softly. Juan's bright eyes stared back at her from the top bunk, and Carlos was wiggling around in the bassinet. Both were up and running.

Julia heard the airplane sound of the Nespresso machine whipping up Alex's coffee. She came into the bedroom and helped Juan get down, then escorted him to the bathroom. The training seat was in place, and he knew what to do. Juan had potty-trained himself at two.

Leaving Juan, she went back into the room to deal with Carlos. His happy smile greeted her from the bassinet as she stood up, holding onto the sides. In Carlos's language, he asked her to pick him up, which she did. Straight to the changing table he went, the five-pound diaper hanging dangerously off his little waist. She quickly cleaned him up and put on a dry diaper. Julia hoped Carlos would follow in his brother's footsteps and potty-train himself at a young age. After taking care of her children, she left them in their bedroom to play while she went to the kitchen to fix breakfast.

Alex was sitting at the table, staring out the window.

"The next diaper is yours," she said, smiling.

He smiled at her. "Oh sure, I get the one right after breakfast. Thanks a lot!" They both laughed.

Alex stopped laughing and, in a serious voice, said, "I figure he will try for us in the next few nights. The front door is too visible from the street, so he'll probably come from the back."

"Why did you say *he*? Don't you think it will be more than one person?"

"There was only one person in the car, and unless he is just a scout, it looks like only one shooter."

"That doesn't make much sense," Julia said.

"It does if this is some kind of personal vendetta, and that's all I can figure out. It must have something to do with the Bloods."

"I thought we left all that behind us, Alex."

"I had hoped so, but sometimes, you just can't outrun your past," he said.

The morning progressed as normal for a Sunday. They had their breakfast, and the boys settled down to watch some cartoons, a treat because Alex and Julia weren't into television much. They sat around talking and playing with the kids, a seemingly normal Sunday.

Raul had his plan. He'd seen the empty back lot that went up to the duplex back doors. The back street was pretty much empty, mostly weed-infested lots and only a few houses widely spaced apart. He'd wait until dark, using that for cover.

He put the Glock on the coffee table, getting ready to disassemble it for cleaning. He was taking no chances.

Alex and Julia had agreed to keep their routines as normal as possible, although they postponed walks with the kids. Alex had asked Mrs. Sojun and her daughter to be on the lookout for any strangers lurking around, but last night, no one had been seen. He figured Sunday or during the week would be better for the shooter, not so many people on the streets.

At 8:00 p.m., Julia and Alex were putting the kids to bed. As was their custom, a bedtime story had been picked out and was ready for the reading. Carlos and Juan were both in the bottom bunk, ready for their story. It was Alex's turn to read, but Julia sat next to him, listening as intently as the kids.

Alex started out, "Once upon a time, long, long ago . . ." When finished, they put the boys in their respective beds and turned out the overhead light. The soft glow of their nightlight threw shadows on the walls. Neither boy had nightmares, and the shadows were not threatening to them.

Julia softly closed the door; Alex was already back in the living room. As she came down the hallway, she heard a soft knocking at the front door. Alex got up, signaling her to stand behind the wall while he opened the door. She held her club ready.

Mrs. Sojun called out, "Alex, Julia, it's me. Rachael saw a gray car parked about three blocks away when she walked home from Rogers."

"Thanks, Mrs. Sojun. Now, you and Rachael lock your doors. I don't want to see you come out until we tell you it is all clear. OK?"

"OK, but you be careful, you two." He heard her footsteps receding on the gravel driveway.

Alex told Julia why he thought the attack would come through the back door. They decided to keep the lights in the living room on until nine-thirty, then turn them off to look like they were going to bed. They'd leave their bedroom light on for a while, then turn it off too. The back door was off the kitchen, and Alex figured the intruder would jimmy the lock and come in through the kitchen straight back to their bedroom. He had no reason to suspect Alex was alert to any danger.

Chapter 38

Julia went into the children's room, a club in hand. The boys were sleeping peacefully, and she settled down on the lower bunk, prepared to defend the kids with her life. She didn't worry about Alex, or at least that's what she told herself. If Alex couldn't stop him or them, then she certainly couldn't, but she wouldn't go down easy.

Alex debated whether to hide outside, keeping the action out there, or attack when he opened the door. The lack of trees for concealment didn't work in his favor, so he opted to wait inside by the door. When the assailant was picking the lock, he would need both hands, and that's when Alex would go for him. If there was more than one of them, he'd disable the first guy and go for the backup. This was the most dangerous part. If the second guy was alert, he could probably shoot Alex before he could get to him. It was a chance he'd have to take. The back door opened out, so if he kicked just as it unlocked, the door should catch the attacker, disabling him, or so was the theory.

He sat in a kitchen chair with the lights off just off to the left of the door. He'd stay like that until it was safe or until morning. Julia and the kids were as safe as he could make them without forcing them to leave. Julia was adamant that leaving was not a choice, and she also vetoed taking the boys to Mrs. Sojun's apartment, where she couldn't protect them.

Alex wasn't used to the waiting game. He'd always preferred to be the one initiating an attack, not waiting for it to happen. This was a different situation, though, and he'd have to deal with it differently. He had a weapon of sorts, a hickory chair leg he had kept for just such an occasion. It wasn't much, but in his hands, it was lethal enough. Of course, the attacker(s) had a gun, so it wasn't exactly an even match. But he had much to lose, and that gave him a mental advantage.

Raul watched the kids' room lights go out, then the living room lights. He could see the glow of their bedroom lights and waited until they also went out. He walked all the way back to the corner and made his way up the half-empty street behind the duplex. He'd seen no one, and fortunately, no dogs were around to sound an alarm.

It was dark, only diffused light coming from streetlights a block away. He didn't like not having trees or cars that would hide his movements, but nobody was nearby, so it didn't really matter. His dark clothing and the black ball cap made him pretty much invisible.

Raul reached the lot at the back of the duplex. Looking around, he started toward the two back doors, knowing their unit was on the left. The building was quiet, with no sounds coming from either unit. He got to the back steps; there were only two. Quietly climbing up, he froze, hearing a sound on his left. His right hand gripped the Glock, still in his coat pocket. He slowly pulled it free and held it at his side. He heard rustling about twelve feet away and caught a glimpse of a straggly cat slinking away into the weeds. Raul relaxed and put the Glock back in his pocket. He'd need two hands to pick the door lock.

He pulled the lockpick from his left pocket, glad he had thought to wear thin gloves. He'd need to be able to feel what he was doing. The plan was to unlock the door, enter the kitchen, and work his way back to their bedroom. He knew their bedroom was at the end, past the kids' room on the right and the bathroom on the left. He'd seen the layout of the duplex in the county records. The property had been a HUD property, so they had the information on file.

He stood on the top step, holding the lockpick up to the key slot and slowly inserted it, holding the doorknob still with his left hand. He didn't see Mrs. Sojun hiding behind the wall of the apartment, watching him. He wiggled the lockpick for a few seconds then. Hearing the click, he quietly pulled the lockpick out of the doorknob to put it back in his coat and pull out the Glock, but before he could do it, the door swung open with tremendous force, knocking him off the steps. Raul was stunned, lying on the ground. That was enough time for Alex to leap out of the house and kick Raul in the face. He went limp.

Raul's gun had fallen out of his pocket onto the ground, and Alex bent down to pick it up. He had misjudged Raul's injuries and was rewarded with a face full of sand and gravel. Blinded momentarily, he stumbled back as Raul leaped up, slicing at Alex with the knife he had strapped to his calf. He caught him across the arm and stomach.

Alex instinctively kicked out, his left foot catching Raul with a glancing blow in the upper thigh. Raul stumbled back a few feet but quickly recovered.

Alex rubbed his eyes, his vision clearing. Now Raul had lost his advantage of surprise, but he had the knife. Both men squared off, and Raul quickly looked around on the ground, trying to see where the gun had fallen.

Alex moved in, feinting a left at Raul's face, which brought his knife hand up to block it. He quickly shifted his weight to his left side to give more power to his right-hand strike. He didn't bother trying to hit Raul in the face but tried to damage Raul's throat with his rigid fingers. His hand glanced off Raul's left arm and, in return, had to deflect Raul's knife from his midsection. He was obviously a good knife fighter, whereas Alex had no experience in this type of battle. He realized he was at a big disadvantage if he let this guy get in close with the knife. He had only one option—take the battle to him.

Alex stepped back, pretending to be afraid of Raul's knife. Raul had a slight smile on his face, seeing Alex backing off, and he immediately attacked. This is what Alex wanted, and instead of backing up to avoid the thrust, he bent forward and twisted, catching the knife between his arm and his side. Then he head-butted Raul in the face, knocking his head back just enough for Alex to use his elbow on his throat. He let the pinned knife arm loose as Raul fell back. Following him back, Alex leaped into the air, hitting Raul in the face with his knee. He felt the nose cartilage break and rode him down to the ground, his body driving the air out of Raul as he landed on his chest.

Raul had dropped the knife, his fingers lifeless. He struggled to take in air through his shattered nose and crushed larynx. Alex knew the fight was over.

He went up the steps to the kitchen and called out to Julia.

"Call 911. It's over." Then he turned back to the man gasping on the ground. "Why, why did you try to kill us? We don't know you, never did anything to you." Raul just looked at him with angry eyes, unable to speak.

CHAPTER 39

The police and ambulance got to their house in minutes. Julia was smart enough to know someone would need medical attention, so she made sure an ambulance was dispatched. The boys never woke up, the two fighters doing their work in silence. Julia had come out of their bedroom into the hallway to call. Then she went through the kitchen and out into the yard.

The attacker was on the ground, gasping for air, and Alex was standing beside him. Alex didn't look too good; blood drenched the front of his shirt and dripped off his left arm, but at least he was standing.

Two officers came around the left side of the duplex with Mrs. Sojun closely followed by two emergency medical technicians. The police officers had their pistols drawn and were covering Alex since he was the one standing up. Julia called out to them, saying she was the one who had called. They asked her name and verified it as the person who had phoned in. Meanwhile, Mrs. Sojun was jabbering in their ear that Alex was the good guy.

The first officer lowered his gun, but the second one didn't. The second officer told his partner that there was a gun and knife on the ground. Not going any closer, the first officer asked Alex if he had any weapons. Alex said no. The officer approached him cautiously.

"Paul, check the guy on the ground and bag the weapons." He was obviously the senior officer. "Have the medics check these guys out." He turned and called dispatch, letting them know what had transpired.

One of the medics kneeled by Raul. He was still gasping and was unable to talk.

"This guy's larynx and nose are crushed. I'm gonna have to do a quick airway traic," he told his partner. "Hold him still." Opening his med kit, he uncased a scalpel and, quickly feeling the vertebrae of Raul's throat and counting them, made a quick incision below the crushed larynx. Raul jumped when the blade bit, but the EMT held him down. Then the medic inserted a plastic tube into the incision. Bloody bubbles came out of the tube, then just a wheezing sound.

"Bandage the tube in place while I check this other guy," he told his partner. He stood, closed his kit, and walked over to Alex. One of the police officers stood by Raul while the medic secured his breathing tube.

The senior officer was talking to Alex when the medic came up. The medic looked at his arm, then asked Alex to pull up his shirt. The stomach wound concerned him more, but they both looked superficial, just painful.

"I'm going to clean both wounds, then bind them. You need to go to the emergency room to get those sewed up," the medic said.

Alex nodded OK.

"I'll make sure of it," Julia said, standing to one side of Alex.

"I recognized Raul Vega. You're lucky to be alive, tangling with him. We're going to have him transported to County Hospital for treatment now. Follow us to County and get those taken care of," he senior officer said, pointing at Alex's wounds. "I'll take your statement there."

Chapter 40

Julia drove Alex to the hospital. Mrs. Sojun was staying at the house with the boys. Alex was hurting but relatively OK.

"Why did he want to hurt us, Alex? I've never seen him before."

"Me either, Julia. He didn't say anything to me back there. Maybe we'll find out more at the police station."

They got to County Hospital and parked in the emergency parking lot. Officer Canon, the senior police officer from the scene, was waiting for them as Alex was admitted.

They put Alex in an observation room; both Julia and Officer Canon were present. A nurse came in, removed the dressings, and put stitches in both wounds. The one on his stomach was angry-looking with jagged edges. The nurse said the knife must have caught in the material. She cleaned and dressed both wounds, and a doctor came in, looked him over, and prescribed antibiotics. He asked if Alex needed any pain medication. Alex said no.

After they had treated Alex, Officer Canon told them he needed the observation room for thirty minutes. The doctor grumbled but said OK. When he had gone, Officer Canon turned to Alex. "OK, let's get your statement. I'll get Mrs. Sojun's tomorrow."

*****

Back home, Alex and Julia thanked Mrs. Sojun and sent her home. The boys never woke up.

"Officer Canon said to call the station tomorrow, and he'd tell us what Raul had said. Then I needed to come in and sign a complaint. They are going to keep that Raul guy locked up for several days while they process his open warrants. Apparently, they're glad to get him."

"I just want to know what this was all about. He was going to hurt our children!" Julia had tears in her eyes.

"I know, baby, I know." He put his arm around her.

The rest of the night was uneventful, but neither of them got much sleep. In the morning, Alex called work and left a message that he wouldn't be in. He had to go to the station for the complaint, and he was anxious to find out if they had learned anything. Julia would stay home with the kids.

At the precinct, he asked to see Officer Canon. They called upstairs, and he came down to collect Alex.

"Come up to my office, Alex, so we can talk." He turned to go up the stairs, Alex following behind him.

"How are you feeling?" he asked, sitting down behind a beat-up wooden desk. He gestured to a chair facing him.

Alex sat down gingerly. "I'm OK," he said, "just a little sore. Did he say anything about last night?" jumping right into his biggest question.

"Nothing yet, and now he is lawyering up."

"What's that mean?" he asked Officer Canon, not understanding.

"Means he won't say anything to us without his lawyer present."

"He can do that?" Alex asked.

"Yep, it's the law. What we do know is that he is tied in with a gang known as the Bloods and has a brother who works down in old El Paso, but that's about it."

"Hmm," Alex said, "do you know his brother's name?"

"Uhh, yes, it's Freddy Vega."

Alex just shook his head, everything making sense now. Raul was the brother of the guy he had killed in old El Paso.

Chapter 41

The attack and arrest of Raul Vega made the papers the next morning. When Alex went to work, the office was buzzing with the news. His old boss called him from Ruidoso Downs to make sure he was OK. Apparently, the news had even gotten that far.

Raul was scheduled for an arraignment two weeks from that Monday. Alex would be the primary witness, and Johnson Construction had provided an attorney to represent him. Alex had no idea what he would do at a hearing. Mrs. Sojun and her daughter were also prosecution witnesses. Alex was having a hard time getting anything done at work. Everyone wanted to talk about Sunday night. Alex just wanted to move on.

Two hundred miles away, a man heard about the attack on the local news. He took a pen off the nightstand and wrote "Alex and Julia Lima" on a piece of paper.

Raul Vega, it turned out, was wanted for several drug-related murders, so it was big news. Now that they had Vega behind bars, police detectives started putting pressure on some of his men, hoping to turn a witness to one of his other crimes. It paid off when Jason Freeman, one of Vega's drug runners, turned state's evidence for a plea deal. He was an eyewitness to a Vega hit seven months before. It looked like Raul was out of business.

Alex tried to ignore all the hoopla. He went to work as normal, came home as normal, and still ran every morning, although sometimes he had to dodge reporters. It had been a week since the arraignment. Raul Vega was held over for trial on one count of murder and one count of attempted murder, but it would take time for the prosecution and defense lawyers to prepare their cases. They had set a trial date almost three months away.

Meanwhile, interest in Alex had died down, allowing him to live an almost normal life. He knew that once they were close to the trial date, it would all start up again. The detectives had interviewed Alex, Julia, Mrs. Sojun, and her daughter Rachael several times, both before and after Vega's defense attorney had them dispositioned. It was obvious to Alex that Vega's defense was based on discrediting the witnesses. That would be difficult with them because what happened was straightforward and corroborated by the police called to the scene. The witness to Vega's earlier murder was another matter. Jason Freeman was a known drug dealer and two-time loser who had spent time in a Texas state prison. His credibility was definitely an issue. Police detectives were desperately trying to find other witnesses to corroborate his story, but so far, they had struck out.

Alex didn't worry about any of that since it had nothing to do with him. He didn't think the Bloods would want to get involved either—too much attention. The only issue in Alex's case is the lack of motive. Nobody knew why Raul had gone after Alex, and he wasn't talking. Neither was Raul. The police were going with the idea that this was a burglary gone wrong, but that was weak because Alex wasn't wealthy and, therefore, a lousy candidate for a home invasion. But it didn't really matter. This case was built on actual events. The defense couldn't dispute the evidence that the weapons and lockpick belonged to Raul; his fingerprints were all over them. Mrs. Sojun would testify that she saw Raul trying to break into the house and then try to kill Alex. She and her daughter would be hard to discredit because she had no reason to lie. Her daughter Rachael would testify that she saw Raul park his car and try sneaking into their backyard.

Chapter 42

"All rise for the Honorable Judge Nelson."

Everyone stood as the judge entered the courtroom.

"Please be seated," the judge said.

Raul Vega was standing between two guards, hands secured in front of him. He looked uninterested in the proceedings. In fact, Alex thought he looked bored. He took his seat at the defense table. One of the guards sat next to him, and the other took his place behind Vega's seat. The jury had been picked with both attorneys arguing their selections. A jury was finally agreed upon, but neither party was happy with the results. The judge asked the bailiff to bring in the jury. Before they sat down, the judge addressed them.

"You and each of you, do you solemnly swear that you will well and truly try this case before you, and a true verdict render, according to the evidence and the law so help you God?" They answered in the affirmative and were seated.

The judge asked the attorneys if they were ready with their opening statements. Both indicated they were ready. The prosecution had the burden of proof to show beyond a reasonable doubt that the defendant was guilty of the specific crimes charged, so he would go first.

The state prosecutor stood, turning to address both the jury and judge. He quickly and clearly laid out an overview of the case, including what the state planned to prove and how they planned to prove it. This was an attempted murder case, so the state prosecutor was especially clear about what evidence they would offer and what witnesses they would call in support of their claims.

When the prosecutor finished, the judge asked the defense attorney to provide his opening statement.

He stood, addressing the jury, as did the prosecutor.

"Good morning, ladies and gentlemen of the jury. My name is John Blakeman, and I, together with my colleagues, represent the defendant Mr. Raul Vega." He pointed Raul out when he mentioned him by name.

"The defendant stands here today wrongly accused of the crime of attempted <u>murder</u>, breaking and entering, and trespass—all very serious offenses. At the end of this trial, we are going to ask you to render a verdict of not guilty, the only appropriate verdict in this case."

When both attorneys had finished their statements and rebuttal, the prosecution was first to call witnesses and present evidence. It would be up to the defense attorney to try and dispute the evidence and discredit the witnesses. First up was Officer Canon, who testified as to the events he witnessed and the evidence that was collected. When it was his turn, the defense attorney tried to dispute the validity of the evidence but could prove no instances of mishandling or chain of custody errors. He didn't try to discredit Officer Canon, feeling that it would be more harmful than helpful. There was nothing in the officer's record that he could use against him.

Each time the prosecutor introduced evidence, the defense would try to have it suppressed, but he was overruled each time. He could tell the judge was getting frustrated, but he was desperate to find something he could defend his client with. He knew coming in that the prosecutor's case was a foregone conclusion, but he had to make as much noise as he could. He knew the gangs were watching the proceedings, and they were a big part of his income. If he didn't at least look good on paper, it could be as bad for him as for Raul.

For three days, the prosecutor presented his evidence and produced his witnesses. At the end of the third day, the prosecution rested, giving the defense attorney his turn.

The defense planned to recall each witness and dispute each piece of evidence. He had been unable to suppress the evidence, so now he had to try to discredit it. He was an experienced litigator, excellent at twisting information to help his case. Unfortunately, there was really nothing to work with here, but he kept spinning the facts until Judge Nelson finally put a stop to it.

"Mr. Williams, this court has heard these same arguments several times now. If you do not have any concrete arguments as to the validity of the evidence or new information regarding the witnesses, I am instructing you to wrap up your presentation, and we will move to closing arguments."

Both parties presented a summary of the case they had presented, and the jury filed out to deliberate. It took less than an hour for the jury to conclude that Raul Vega was guilty of all three counts.

As Judge Nelson read the jury's findings, Vega's disinterested expression never changed. As the judge dismissed the jury and then the court, Raul was led back to his cell to await sentencing. Alex and Julia and the Sojuns returned home.

Raul Vega was sentenced to nineteen years in prison for second-degree attempted murder, criminal trespass, and breaking and entering.

Alex read the story in the local newspaper, relieved that it was over. Vega was still scheduled to be tried for murder in the other case, and apparently, the detectives had found two more corroborating witnesses, probably because Vega was found guilty and was off the streets. It looked like Raul Vega would spend the rest of his life in jail if he was lucky.

*****

Meanwhile, the man read the article again. None of the articles ever mentioned Alex and Julia's home address, but that was no issue. It took seconds to look it up on the Internet.

He smiled to himself. *Looks like a road trip is coming up shortly*, he thought.

Chapter 43

Juan ran behind the tree, waiting for Julia to count to ten. "Ready or not, here I come," she called out.

Juan couldn't help but giggle, loving this game. Julia had to laugh, pretending not to know where he was hiding. After looking in different spots, she snuck up behind Juan and grabbed him. He let out a surprised squeal.

"OK, your turn to count and then find me," she said.

"K, Mommy," he said. "Hide behind that tree, and I'll try to find you."

Alex and Carlos were over in the grass, playing worm. They wiggled around on the lawn, pretending they didn't have arms or legs. This was a game Juan had come up with, but he was busy playing hide-and-seek with Mom, so it was just Dad and son. Alex rolled around for a little while, then stood up, brushing the grass off.

"Come on, big guy, let's see what they're doing." He picked Carlos up and swung him around in a circle, Carlos's squeals of delight echoing in the playground. A little dizzy himself, Alex stopped spinning him and started walking toward Julia.

As he walked up, he saw Julia crouching behind a tree and Juan counting. When he finished, he started looking around even though he had told Julia where to hide.

Alex waved at him and pointed at the tree. Juan smiled and ran over to it, tagging his mom and laughing.

"Cheater," she called out to Alex, smiling.

They stayed another hour playing with the children. A neighbor had brought her children over, and the boys were happy to have someone of their own age. Carlos didn't really care; he just crawled around, happy just to be outside, but Juan and the girl Janie got along well. They weren't the same age, but Juan spoke more like a five-year-old than a three-year-old, so it was OK since Janie was five. Like most Hispanic kids, both spoke English and Spanish, and their conversations usually mixed the two languages. Saran's boy Roberto was seven and felt he was too old to play with the younger kids, so he went off to hang out under the trees. Carlos found him there. To Roberto's credit, he didn't try to run Carlos off; he just ignored him, which was fine with Carlos. He was busy trying to find a grasshopper or caterpillar. Julia was afraid of what he would do with it if he found one. A lot of items ended up in his mouth, so she kept an eye on him.

The boys were getting tired, about ready to head home. Julia grabbed Carlos just before he tried to eat a particularly juicy-looking frog; Alex picked Juan up. They headed home, carrying both contented boys. Alex saw a late-model Lincoln parked in the driveway in front of Mrs. Sojun's house. It was interesting only because Mrs. Sojun didn't usually hang out with people who drove Lincolns. As they got closer to Mrs. Sojun's front door, it opened, and a man came out with Mrs. Sojun.

She called to Alex. "Alex, can you come over for a minute? Mr. Padiea would like a word."

Alex looked the man over; sure, he had never seen him before. He turned to Julia. "Can you take Juan in? I'll go see what he wants."

"I hope it's not more crap about the trial," Julia said, eyeing the well-dressed stranger. "He looks like trouble."

"That's what I love about you. You're so welcoming," he said, smiling. Alex handed Juan to her and turned to go over to Mrs. Sojun's. If the guy had been a reporter or somebody else just looking for information, Mrs. Sojun would have given him the bum's rush.

He walked up to the man standing on the steps. "I'm Alex Lima. How can I help you?"

"Well, actually, son, you're not Alex Lima now, are you?"

Chapter 44

Mr. Padiea and Alex sat at Mrs. Sojun's small kitchen table while she brewed some tea for her guests. Mr. Padiea explained to Alex that he was the estate attorney for the late Trina Gonzales from Ruidoso Downs. He was here looking for Mr. Gonzales's heir, and he thought Alex might be him. Alex just looked at him, unsure of what to say. Mr. Gonzales went on.

"Mr. Gonzales had a wife and son that he brought with him from Mexico about sixteen years ago. Circumstances forced him to leave his family and prevented him from contacting them. Mr. Gonzales left a detailed journal about his early years here that he said would explain everything to his heir. He also told me how to identify his wife and son if I should find them."

When Mr. Padiea paused, Alex said, "What makes you think I might be his son?"

"Well, you're the right age, the right race, and when my firm checked you out, we found you have no history prior to coming to work for Johnson Construction. We also know his family was in El Paso, at least when he first came to the United States. I could find no reference to his wife at all. If it hadn't been for the articles about the trial, you wouldn't even have been a consideration."

"I'm sorry, Mr. Padiea, I'm afraid you have the wrong person." Alex stood up, ready to leave.

"One thing, Mr. Lima, Mr. Gonzales said there was something he gave to his son that would prove who he was. I know what that was, but do you have any idea what it might be?" Alex knew immediately what that item was.

"I'm sorry, Mr. Padiea. I really have no interest in this matter. I wish you luck in your search." Alex walked out of the duplex.

Back at his own house, he told Julia what had happened. They were sitting in the living room, the boys both napping. Julia looked at him.

"I don't understand, Alex. You act like you don't want to know if this Mr. Gonzales was your father."

Alex didn't answer right away. "I'm not sure I do. I guess it's better if he's dead. I have a lot of anger toward him for leaving us in a strange country with nothing." He paused, thinking about his next words. "Maybe it's best if I don't know why he did it, why he abandoned us." He looked at Julia. "What if he was some kind of monster? I mean, what other kind of person would leave their family to die?"

"Alex, this has eaten at you for over twenty years. I think you need to know the truth so you can put it behind you." She took him in her arms. "Just look at you. Think about what you've been through and what you've become. If he is your father, he couldn't have been a monster and create a son like you." Tears glistened in her eyes. "You need to find out the truth."

The following Monday, Alex called Mr. Padiea at his office in Ruidoso Downs. They set a time and place to meet. Mr. Padiea asked him to come to the office because he had the files there and they couldn't leave the office. Alex agreed. That night, he didn't sleep, too nervous about the meeting.

The two-hour drive up Highway 10 was uneventful. Ruidoso Downs was where Mr. Padiea had an office, and that's where the file on Mr. Gonzales was. Ruidoso Downs was a small town, and finding the law office was easy. Alex pulled into their parking lot and shut off the car. He was nervous and was still not completely convinced that this was the right move. He felt for the three marbles in his pocket. His office manager thought he had gone crazy when she saw him break the paperweight with a hammer. Somehow, this seemed right.

Alex got out of the car and went up to the door. Inside, he told the receptionist that he had an appointment with Mr. Padiea. She asked his name and then told him that the attorney was waiting for him. She got up and showed him into the office.

The attorney was sitting behind a large desk with several stacks of papers scattered on top. The office was lined with bookshelves filled with dozens of hard-bound books, case histories, law doctrines, Spanish and English dictionaries, and what looked to Alex like a bunch of college law books. It was obviously there to impress clients, not serve any real purpose.

"Alex, I'm glad you decided to come," the bespeckled attorney said, jumping up from behind the desk and reaching out to shake his hand. "Please, sit here." He pointed to one of the two chairs facing the desk. Alex sat down in the chair he had indicated, and Mr. Padiea sat back down behind his desk. Sweeping some papers to the side, he opened the top drawer of the desk and took out a manila folder. He put it in front of him on the desktop. It was about an inch thick, and Alex could see that besides stacks of loose papers, there was a thin book in the folder.

"So, as I told you when we met, Mr. Lima, I represent a client who recently passed away. Part of his last will and testament included specific instructions on what to do in the event of his demise. The client, Mr. Gonzales, had been ill for quite some time. Our firm was hired to create the will under his explicit instructions and to act on his behalf as administrators for his estate. We concluded the probate process almost a year ago." He stopped talking for a minute and seemed to be carefully thinking about his next words.

"Besides the instructions on overseeing his estate, our client gave us directions on how to locate his heirs. These directions were fairly broad, only pinpointing the age of the male heir and his birthdate, the client's wife's maiden name and town she and her son were born in, her approximate age, and the city where they were last in residence. Based on this information, we discovered fourteen people who could possibly be the client's relatives. Unfortunately, all fourteen were ruled out during our investigations, and until we discovered you, we had no other candidates."

"I'm sorry, Mr. Padiea, I doubt I am who you are looking for. I don't really remember what town in Mexico I was born in or my mother's maiden name."

"I understand that, Mr. Lima, and I'm not surprised. You would have been very young when you came to the United States. What about your mother? I'm sure she would recognize our client's picture even though it has been many years since she has seen him. Could you arrange for us to interview her?"

"I'm afraid that won't be possible. My mother passed away when I was young."

"I'm sorry for your loss, Mr. Lima."

Alex thanked him.

"We do have the ability to match DNA. This was prepared prior to Mr. Gonzales's death."

"I'm sorry, Mr. Padiea, I'm not really interested in going any further in this process. Sorry to have wasted so much of your time." Alex stood up, preparing to leave the office.

"Just do me one courtesy, Mr. Lima. As I said, Mr. Gonzales left a journal that could only be given to his son. As a favor to me, would you just look at that journal before you go? I'll just step out of the office while you look it over. It should only take you a few minutes. If you are still not interested in pursuing this, I will understand and bother you no more." He slid the folder over toward Alex, got up, and went out his office door, closing it behind him.

Alex stood there staring at the folder, then sat back down and pulled the folder to him.

Chapter 45

Alex Lima thanked the orderly at the clinic. The health worker gathered the vial of blood taken from Alex and left the small room. Alex pulled his sleeve down over the elastic bandage holding the gauze over the small puncture wound. He got up and went down the hallway past the receptionist and out the door.

He got in his car, preparing to drive the four miles to his house. He sat for a moment, thinking about the journal and what it had meant to him. There was no doubt in his mind that Mr. Gonzales had been his father. He understood now why his father had disappeared and had never tried to find them. He also knew now why the three marbles were supposed to be so valuable.

At home, he sat with Julia on their sofa. Julia also knew the answers that Alex had learned. She took his hand, and they both silently looked out the window for a few minutes. Neither of them spoke.

Finally, Julia turned to Alex. "I need to go get the kids from Mrs. Sojun. You going to be OK?"

Alex nodded yes, still lost in thought.

The journal that Mr. Gonzales had left was a shock to Alex. After the first five pages, he knew in his heart that this man was his father. Mr. Gonzales, or Trina Gonzales by his full name, had been a Mexican drug agent. He and his family were living in Chilopa because his unit was part of the Mérida Initiative with the United States, which focused specifically on the cartels. In Mexico, crimes are seldom investigated, and there is no way of knowing if the thousands of deaths each year are attributed to organized crime, the police, or the cartels. Trina Gonzales was asked to infiltrate the Sinaloa Cartel in Chilapa, Mexico, one of the busiest production and distribution centers for the cartel. They hoped to link organized crime to the multitude of murders occurring in Chilapa. When Trina accepted the assignment, he was not aware that his wife was pregnant. By the time he found out, it was too late to stop.

On August 4, 1999, the Mexican government told Trina Gonzales that the Beltrán brothers had been tipped off about a government agent infiltrating their ranks at the Chilopa production site. They knew little about the agent, except that he had a wife and young son. Trina was told to get himself and his family out as fast as possible. Mexican authorities would contact a smuggler who worked with them to take the family to the United States.

Trina knew that it was only a matter of time before they figured out who he was. By then, he and his family would be across the border. Trina also knew that fleeing to the United States was not enough to make them safe. The cartel had many members in the United States. The only way he could keep his family safe was to leave them in El Paso, hoping that the cartel would follow him and not look for them. Alex was too young to understand why he was leaving. All he could do was give him something to remember him by. Trina hoped that as Alex got older, he would look at the three marbles and think of his father.

For twenty years, Trina Gonzales had a productive life in the United States. He never got over the guilt of deserting his family, but he had made peace with it. So many times, he had wanted to go to El Paso and find them and make sure they were OK. But he was still on the cartel's radar, and signs that they were looking for him were everywhere. He had testified about the killings that he had knowledge of. However, Mexican justice was a very slow process, and when the authorities were finally ready to move on the brothers, they were found dead in one of the canyons outside of Chilopa.

Five years after leaving his family, Trina felt it was now safe enough to sneak into El Paso and try to find them. On a clear September Tuesday morning, Trina drove his Blazer down to Old Town to find his family. For several hours he walked the old, deserted streets, trying to find anyone that would help him. Finally, he cornered a young boy and showed him a picture of his wife and son. The boy's name was Eric, and he was terrified of Trina. When he realized the man wasn't ICE and was looking for somebody else, not him, he looked at the picture again. He recognized the woman and boy right away, although the boy was much older now.

Trina pointed to the woman in the picture and said, "Donde?" ("Where?")

Eric looked at her picture and replied, "Muerto." ("Dead.")

Trina sighed and pointed to the picture of Alex. "Donde?" he said. Eric was silent for a minute, then said, "Ido," ("Gone.")

Trina spent the rest of the day going up and down the streets of old El Paso. Mostly he saw kids who ran and hid as soon as they saw him. He was able to question two or three more kids, but they said they didn't know either of them. Disappointed, he walked back to his car, planning to keep coming back until he found Alex.

Over the years, Trina made many more trips to old El Paso, but he was never able to find anything out about Alex or about his wife's death. He figured the kid Eric was right; Alex had left old El Paso somehow. He would keep looking but finding him was going to be hard. US authorities were helping. An alert had been put out on Alex, but Trina didn't know what name he was using, so they had very little to go by. Hundreds of young Mexican boys his age lived in El Paso, and he didn't even know if Alex was still in that town. Trina ran ads in the personal section of the *El Paso Times* for several months and got many responses, but they were all from people trying to make money on him. Finally, he gave up and just hoped for the best for his son.

Alex put the journal down, not bothering to finish it. He wasn't interested in his father's life after he deserted them. Alex tossed the folder and journal back on the desk, got up, and went out.

Chapter 46

The attorney called Alex eleven days after the DNA test was performed.

"Alex, I'd like to set up a meeting in my office and go over the results of the test," Padiea said over the phone.

"Why don't you just tell me the results and save me a trip?" Alex said, a little put-off that the attorney seemed to be stalling.

"Sorry, Alex, I am required to meet with you in person to go over the results," he said.

"Required by who, the law?" he asked.

"No, by our client. He left explicit instructions on how to proceed, and I am required by law to follow those instructions. How about Monday morning? Your wife is welcome to attend also."

On Monday, Alex and Julia drove to the attorney's office. Alex assumed the test was positive since he had read the journal. The DNA results really didn't matter to him. The estate meant nothing to him. Julia had urged him to go, hoping that this meeting would put the whole issue behind him. Alex had already decided not to change his name to Gonzales.

They walked in the door, and the same receptionist got up from her desk and took them to the attorney's office. Julia looked around, more impressed by all the books than Alex was. They sat in the two chairs facing the desk and waited for Mr. Padiea. They didn't have long to wait.

The attorney came in with another man. "Alex and Julia, this is Mr. Bower. He was a long-time friend and business associate of your father. Yes, Alex, I said 'father,' but you already knew that from reading the journal. I saw your face when you left my office that day. The DNA test just confirmed it for us."

"So why are we here?" Alex said. "We have no interest in his estate. It can all be donated to charity."

"Alex, I was your father's friend for many years. You need to know that he never gave up trying to find you," Mr. Bower said.

"Your father was a hero who sacrificed his family to help save thousands of people from the drugs coming from Mexico," Bower said. "You should be very proud of what he did for his country and for the United States."

Alex just looked at him; then he said, "I'm not proud of the man who left his wife and child to live or die in the streets of El Paso. I'm not proud of the man who had to sneak his family out of Mexico so they wouldn't be killed, nor am I proud of the man who let an eleven-year-old boy put his dead mother in a gas furnace to keep the rats from chewing on her body. No, I'm not proud of the man who didn't care about us enough to even look for us for five years. I'm sorry, Mr. Padiea, we're leaving." He stood up abruptly, pulling Julia up also.

"Please, Alex, just hear us out. This is about a lot more than money."

"You heard what I said. Donate his estate to some charities. I have no interest in it. Send me whatever papers I need to sign, and I'll sign them and send them back." He didn't stop walking to the door.

"But, Alex, what about . . ." Alex didn't hear the rest; he was already out of the office, closing the door behind him.

Once in the car, Julia turned to him. "Alex," she said, but he cut her off.

"I really don't want to talk about it now, Julia." He started the car and pulled out of the parking lot. It was a silent ride back home.

The attorney kept calling Alex, but he never picked up or returned the messages. Nothing had come in the mail for Alex to sign, so it must not have been much of a problem with the estate. Alex and Julia returned to their lives, putting the past behind them. Two weeks later, a car pulled up in their driveway. Julia had just finished the dinner dishes. Alex was reading in the living room. He heard the car pull up and got up to look out the window. He didn't recognize the car.

"Someone's here, Julia. Watch the boys for a minute." They never stop being careful about strangers. Alex went to the door when he heard the knock. Two people stood on the steps, and he immediately recognized Mr. Bower. He didn't know the girl.

"Mr. Bower," Alex said, shaking the proffered hand. "You could have just sent the papers," he said, assuming that was why he was here. He looked at the girl curiously.

"That's not why I'm here, Alex. You didn't read all of the journal, did you?" It was a statement, not a question.

"No, what was the point? I had no interest in his life without us." Mr. Bower looked disappointed.

"Well, Alex, let me introduce you to Isabella. She brought something to show you." The girl took a step closer and put out her closed hand to Alex. When she opened it, three marbles lay in her palm.

ABOUT THE AUTHOR
JAN R. MCDONALD

Businessman, Author, and World Traveler, Jan R McDonald is a natural born storyteller.

From bedtime stories to monthly newsletters to his grandchildren, Mr. McDonald combines real life experiences with fictional situations that create entertaining and absorbing reads.

Retired and now living in Florida, Jan R. McDonald has borrowed from his real-life experiences to create humorous, fictional and non-fiction adventures. *3 Marbles* is the second of Mr. McDonald's fiction novels.